"The last thing I wanted to do was hurt you."

He continued stroking her. As he soothed away her worries, she felt a warmth growing inside her. A shiver of anticipation trembled up her spine as his head inclined slowly to hers, and she read the intention in his eyes. He was going to kiss her, but, like a gentleman, he was waiting to see if she objected. She lifted her warm lips to his. The reaction was like a spark to tinder. After the first light touch, his arms crushed her against his hard chest. As his lips firmed, bruising hers in a ruthless kiss, she felt as if her lungs had collapsed, sending her heart up to pound in her throat.

Pent-up passion flooded through her like a tidal wave as she returned every ardent pressure. . . .

DAMSEL IN DISTRESS

Joan Smith

FAWCETT CREST • NEW YORK

A Fawcett Crest Book
Published by Ballantine Books
Copyright © 1995 by Joan Smith

Library of Congress Catalog Card Number: 94-94653

ISBN 0-449-22278-0

Manufactured in the United States of America

First Edition: February 1995

10 9 8 7 6 5 4 3 2 1

Chapter One

Caroline, Countess of Winbourne, came tripping down the grand staircase of her mansion in Berkeley Square, ran into the Gold Saloon, and performed a graceful curtsey. Daintily lifting the tails of her skirt, she said, "How do I look, Georgie? Shall I set a new fashion with this gown, or is it too outré?"

It would have seemed odd to any bystander, of whom there was none, to hear an out-and-outer like Lady Winbourne ask for fashion advice from a spinster of fifty-odd years who had not had a new gown made up for herself in a decade. Lady Georgiana Eden's lean body was encased in an exceedingly plain blue sarsenet gown, and her gray hair was tightly bound under an aging silk cap with lace lappets.

Georgiana's rheumy eyes twinkled as they surveyed Caroline. No one had ever bothered giving Georgiana a nickname before. It had a dégagé sound to it that did not suit her in the least, which was perhaps why she liked it. She noticed Caroline was wearing violet again, not in half mourning for her late husband, but to match the unusual shade of her eyes, which were her chief claim to beauty. They were large, wide-set, and still bore the lustre of youth. A raven tousle of curls provided the perfect foil for her ivory complexion, suggesting a delicately carved cameo. Added to her manifold charms were an energy and irresistible liveliness that could still enchant, even on those occasions when they outran the bounds of propriety. She was altogether an enchanting creature, Georgiana thought, without a single tinge of jealousy. She was as proud of Caro as if the girl were her own daughter.

"Very nice, my dear. You will knock their bonnets off, as Julian was used to say."

"You haven't seen the best part," Caroline said, performing a pirouette to show off the low back of her gown.

A little gasp issued from Georgiana's throat, followed by a simulated cough to hide her first sound of surprise. The gown really was very low-cut at the back, a good foot lower than any other lady would be wearing. It was laced to prevent it from falling off her body entirely, but a good deal of flesh was revealed between the x's of the lace. In fact, the lacing added to the daringness of the gown by suggesting a corset. But there, Caro had a lovely back, so straight and trim, with a natural beauty mark just off center toward the bottom. Why should she not show herself off if it gave her pleasure? Other ladies displayed the half of their bosoms, which was much naughtier of them. She noticed that Caro's gown was not cut particularly low in front. It allowed only a tantalizing glimpse of her breasts.

The girl was a strange mixture of daring and modesty. Her conversation was occasionally "fast," even bordering on the broad at times. Her romantic antics provided society with a good many minor scandals, but to the best of Lady Georgiana's knowledge, Caro had not actually taken a lover yet, and Julian had been dead for three years. She winced to remember that she had warned her brother he was mad to marry a chit two decades younger than himself—and out of a provincial vicarage to boot. But she had been wrong. The two

2

had remained passionately in love until the day Julian took a tumble from his mount and broke his neck.

"He died as he lived, at full gallop," Caro had said, blinking back her tears. "He would not cavil with the manner of his passing. Oh, but I cavil at the timing of it. How shall we go on without him, Georgie?" Then, after the funeral guests had left and they were alone, Caro broke down and sobbed for the first time.

Georgie could offer no consolation but only a reminder that Caro and Julian had enjoyed seven wonderful years together, deprived of nothing but the son they both wanted so badly. Georgiana felt the fault was to be placed in Julian's dish. He had not managed to father an heir by his first wife either. Pity, for it meant the title and estate fell to Cousin Jeremy, Julian being the only male in the immediate family, but at least there was plenty of money.

Julian had begged Caro on his deathbed not to let his death deter her from enjoying a full life, and she had promised that she would try not to. It was for this reason that she had not prolonged her public mourning unduly. Only Georgiana knew that the private grief still continued. Julian's portrait hung at the foot of Caro's bed, where she said good morning to it each day, and even whispered a few details of her evening when she returned at night. When she went to the Rosary, her country estate, at the end of the Season, the portrait went with her. Caroline had spent a year at the Rosary after Julian's death. There, tending the rose gardens that gave the estate its name, she had come to some sort of terms with her loss. At the end of a year, she had returned to London for the Season, as she would have done had Julian lived. He had left her the mansion in Berkeley Square, the country house, and ten thousand a year besides. Pretty good for a provincial miss whose face was her fortune, folks said.

Ten years before, Julian had brought his seventeen-year-old bride to London, where he had dressed her in the first style of fashion, polished her country manners, and proudly presented her at court and to society, where she had been an immediate hit. The ton had been bored with the Season's crop of debs, and delighted in Caro's occasional lapses into rusticity. When Beau Brummell proclaimed her an original, the seal was set on her reputation. Julian's elder sister, Georgiana, had lived with them from the beginning, acting as Caro's companion, instructress in social matters, and, upon Julian's death, her best friend.

"I do not mean to flaunt myself," Caro said, looking at her violet gown, "but only to let my shawl slip from time to time. I wager Emily Cowper will be wearing something similar by next week."

"I shouldn't be a bit surprised. So you are off to the gaming hell. Don't forget to lose two hundred pounds for me."

"I have our money in my reticule. I plan to lose five hundred. I hope it does not take too long, for I want to have time left over to dance. Life is so contrary; when I try to lose money, I seem to keep winning. The first year Julian and I held the gambling night, I won three thousand pounds, and had to play until two in the morning to lose it all again."

The gaming night had become, by tradition, the opening salvo of the Season, as the king's garden party on June fourth was its finale. It had been Julian's idea to catch the ton while its pockets were full, and they were in a good mood. The event had originally been held at Winbourne House, but as the crowd increased to unmanageable proportions, it had been moved to the old Boar and Castle Hostelry and Posting House on Oxford Street. This was no elegant establishment, but as Julian knew, the ton liked to go slumming from time to time. The proceeds went to his and Caro's favorite charity: a home for orphans. Like so many things in the Winbournes' life, the gaming night had been a bit scandalous at first, but as it was carried out under the strictest rules, and as it always raised at least twenty-five thousand pounds for charity, it had become not only acceptable, but virtually de rigueur. The Prince Regent himself attended when he was in town.

It had been Caro's idea to add a ball and a fine supper afterward, to repay the crowd for donating so much money. "In that way, people will still enjoy themselves," she pointed out.

"And besides, you would rather dance than gamble," Julian had added with a knowing smile.

Caro felt a little guilty leaving Georgiana alone. "Why do you not come with me?" she suggested. "I know you do not care for gambling, but you are not too old to stand up and jig it, Georgie."

Georgiana laughed at the mental image of her shaking her poor old racked limbs. "I am well past it, my dear, but you have a good time. Have a lovely time, for as long as you can. You'll be old soon enough, like me."

She spoke with a surprising vehemence, and meant every word. Lord, how her mama had bamboozled her, putting her in a straitjacket with a hundred foolish admonitions. "Young ladies must not put themselves forward. Young ladies must not flirt, or tease, or be alone with a gentleman, or ever be vulgar." But it was the "vulgar" ladies who had the good times, and got a husband in the end, too, while the proper ladies like herself moldered into old age on the shelf, without even the solace of memories to warm their cold nights.

"Oh, Georgie, you are not old!" Caro scolded. "You know perfectly well you can outwalk me in the country, and sit a mount better than any lady I know."

Georgie sniffed in satisfaction. This was true, and a great consolation, but she knew it was a smiling face and a flashing eye that got a lady a husband. Never mind, she had her little consolations. A bottle of Madeira and a novel from the Minerva Press would be her evening's entertainment. A gothic novel for a gothic lady.

"How long I shall be able to keep it up is another matter," she said. "Who is escorting you this evening, Caro?"

Caroline had gone to the mirror to adjust her hair. "Newt," she said over her shoulder.

It was Caroline's custom to begin each Season on her cousin's arm. As the Season progressed, she would gather around her a court of interested and interesting gentlemen. One of these years she would probably marry one of them. She had nearly come to the sticking point two or three times, but always the memory of Julian intruded, and she suddenly found the gentleman too loud, or too stiff-rumped, too dull or too rakish. At times she wondered if Julian was the only man she could ever love. Lately she had become aware that time was pushing hard at her back. She was twenty-seven. Her friends all had their nurseries started. Some of them had grown children. Her friends had been Julian's friends, and many of them were a deal older than she. She wanted children. As she matured, she realized that life had little meaning without a husband and family.

The door knocker sounded, followed by the heavy tread of Crumm, the butler, striding to the door. The scuffling sounds that ensued suggested two men were sparring. Crumm had been a bruiser before he took up buttling. He bore many tokens of his years in the ring: a broken nose, a twisted ear, and a sprinkling of scars amongst them. Caro could not remember what mischief Julian had been up to at the time, that he required a butler capable of ejecting unwanted guests by fisticuffs, if necessary. In any case, Crumm had long been established as a part of the household.

"No need to announce me, Crumm," Mr. Newton said, and sauntered in, chewing at the knuckles he had bruised on Crumm's hard chin. He made a lumpish bow in the ladies' direction, sat down with a sigh, and said, "Well, here I am."

Alfred Newton was not a famous conversationalist. He had two interests in life—horses and finding a wife, in that order. For as long as Caro had known him, and she had known him from the egg, he had been horse-mad. It was only when she came to London with Julian that she learned Newt had progressed to wanting a wife. To this end, he had new jackets made up every Season, each made by a famous tailor, and each looking worse than the last. Beau Brummell once asked him how he achieved such unusual dishabille, whether he slept in his clothes, or was setting a new style by having them specially made prewrinkled.

Never suspecting an insult, Newt had replied without blinking, "Neither one. I just put them on and there the wrinkles are. Can't help you. Sorry."

Besides his ill-fitting jackets, he was cursed with a short, portly figure, a shaggy head of snuff-colored hair, a round, pink face that belonged on a dissolute cherub, and a pair of blue eyes inclined to protrude from his head.

Caro noticed none of this. She looked and saw her cousin and dearest friend, who was like a brother to her. "Would you like a glass of wine, Newt, or shall we leave now?" she asked.

"Just as you like. It is no odds to me." He examined his bruised knuckles, flexed them, and winced with the pain. "A bit of breakage there, I shouldn't be surprised. Don't like to leave my bloods standing

7

in the street long. There will be plenty to drink at the party. Let us go."

Caroline arranged her wrap, gave Georgiana a quick kiss on the cheek, said, "Don't wait up for me," and they were off.

As they left, Georgiana heard Newt say, "Where is it we are going, Caro? Ah, gaming night. I knew there was some reason why I was carrying so much blunt."

Georgiana shook her head, then rose and went off to the small parlor that was her private lair. She was soon having all the excitement she could endure, vicariously, through the trials of Drusilla Gascoyne. Despite her Spartan upbringing and lack of vulgarity, Drusilla was about to land herself an Adonis of royal blood. Only in fiction!

Chapter Two

The management of gaming night had been given over to professionals at Julian's death. For the year of Caro's mourning she had not attended at all, and although she still took an active part in drumming up business, she was not required to act as hostess. She entered by means of a paid ticket, like everyone else. At nine o'clock the gaming room already held a good crowd. The gentlemen's black jackets predominated, interspersed with the brighter hues of ladies' gowns and the sparkle of jewelry. A forest of feathers rose from the older ladies' turbans to flirt dangerously with the chandeliers overhead. The buzz of high society at play rose to the rafters. There were tables for faro, macao, and whist, but the largest group hovered around the roulette table.

"What's your pleasure?" Newt asked Caroline.

"My pleasure is dancing, but first I must lose my money. The roulette wheel for me. I don't know how to play faro or macao, and whist takes too long."

"You don't know how to play whist either," Newt told her. "As to faro, nothing to it. You just bet on what order the cards will turn up in. You see, the banker—"

"You go ahead, Newt. I know you like faro. But mind you don't win!"

"It is a rare night when I win at cards. Lose my shirt is more like it."

Caro bought her counters, choosing the hundred-

9

pound denomination to hasten her losses. She eased her way through the throng, smiling and greeting friends as she progressed toward an open place at the end of the table. The croupier announced, *"Faites vos jeux,"* and Caro put one counter on seven, her lucky number. The wheel was spun round and round, with other bettors placing their counters. As the wheel slowed, the racket around the table subsided to tense silence. The croupier called, *"Rien ne va plus."* No more bets were allowed as the wheel slowed, finally stopping at number seven. The croupier called, *"Sept, rouge, passe, impair.* Seven, red, high, odd." He raked in the losing bets and paid out counters to the winners.

"Oh dear, I have won!" Caro exclaimed, as he shoved a pile of chips at her.

"En plein, madam, thirty-five to one. Congratulations."

She was the largest winner at the table, and with a bet of one hundred pounds, she had won three thousand five hundred pounds.

"Let it ride," she said, hoping to lose it all so that she might proceed to the ballroom soon.

"Oh, madam! *Ça n'est pas possible!* If you win again, you would break the bank," the croupier explained. "Over one hundred thousand pounds. There is a limit of one hundred on *en plein* bets."

"What are *en plein* bets?" she asked.

"Bets placed on an individual number, that pay thirty-five to one."

"Oh. Could I put one counter on each of the numbers?"

The more experienced bettors in the throng moaned. "In that manner, madam, you are hardly betting at all," the croupier explained. "One of the numbers must win; the other thirty-four will lose. You will win back your thirty-five counters, and lose thirty-four."

10

"At this rate, I shall be here all night," she grumbled, and placed one counter on each of the first five numbers. The wheel turned, stopping at number five. She won again, thirty-five more counters.

A little stir began to move around the table. "Caro is winning," was whispered from ear to ear. Others in the room who had not yet chosen their method of losing their money were drawn to the roulette table.

The excitement lent a sparkle to Caro's eyes and a rosy flush to her cheeks. It was fun to win so much money, even if she couldn't in good conscience keep it. She clapped her hands and laughed, "I am rich!" while pushing counters quite at random onto various numbers.

A distinguished gentleman advanced to the table, drawn by the chattering. He found a place across the table from Caro and observed her with interest. He was familiar with the flushed face and fevered eye of the inveterate gambler, and assumed Caroline's excitement was due to gambling fever. A pity, but then, from what he had heard of Countess Winbourne, it was no better than he expected. A bit of a wild filly—but deuced pretty. His eyes roamed slowly, appreciatively, over her eager face and jet black hair, then down the column of her throat to her creamy shoulders, then lower to the swell of incipient bosoms. Very pretty indeed! Not one of those full-blown, voluptuous women, yet more than a pocket Venus. Not aging and worldly-wise, yet not a dewy-eyed deb. In a word—perfect.

He observed her for a few minutes while she placed her bets quite at random, sometimes betting on both black and red, at other times placing a hundred-pound counter on five or ten individual numbers. A scatterbrained creature! Her luck had turned; instead of raking in counters, she watched them being raked away by the croupier. When she had lost over two thousand pounds, the newly arrived gentleman worked his way to her side to try to talk her away from the table. He knew she was a widow, and assumed she could ill afford such heavy losses.

"Lady Winbourne," he said with a bow more businesslike than graceful. "Determined to lose your fortune, are you?"

At the sound of his deep voice, she glanced up to see a pair of cool gray eyes, set in a swarthy face, topped with straight black hair. A slash of dark eyebrows and a strongly chiseled nose lent a proud air to his face. The full, sensuous lips seemed at odds with the rest of him. His broad shoulders were sheathed in a jacket of exquisite tailoring. In his intricately arranged cravat sat a large cabochon ruby. The Marquess of Dolmain! Now, what the devil was he doing here? Quite a feather in the committee's cap to have got him to come. He seldom festooned these social events with his presence. He was extremely eligible. A bachelor—well, widower—of a certain age, good character, excellent fortune. She felt her interest quicken. She lifted her lustrous violet eyes and smiled demurely. Lord Dolmain returned the smile, with a slight inclination of his head.

Caroline found his stern face was greatly improved by a smile. Although she had known him to speak to for a decade, he had never been one of Julian's set. It had seemed odd that, while Julian spoke of him as a "youngster," he was a decade older than herself. Dolmain was a more serious sort of gentleman than her husband. She knew he was a political animal, holding some prestigious post in the government. Horse Guards, was it?

"As you see, I am rapidly running through my fortune," she replied nonchalantly. "It is all for a good cause. Are you not betting, milord?"

"Certainly I am. That is why I am here."

"Then place your bet, sir."

He placed a ten-pound counter on 16–17, *à cheval*, and lost. Caro placed one counter on each of the last five numbers, and also lost. They repeated the procedure, using different combinations and numbers, and lost again. Her pile of counters was rapidly diminishing.

"Why do you not switch to ten-pound counters?" he suggested.

"Because it is ten times more exciting this way," she replied.

He saw the glitter in her violet eyes, and felt a stab of anger. "And ten times more risky," he said curtly.

She tossed her head in dismissal of such caviling. "That is what gambling is all about, *n'est-ce pas?* I like a risk. Are you afraid to play more deeply?" she taunted. "It is all for a good cause."

It had been Dolmain's experience that a gambler could always find a reason—or an excuse. Their luck was running tonight, or if it was not, then obviously their luck was about to turn. Marie had been the same. Lady Winbourne reminded him somewhat of his late wife. She had the same beautiful, impertinent shoulders, and that same lively manner, cavalier, not taking life too seriously. He felt a strong interest, and hardly knew whether it was attraction or repulsion. In any case, the lady was certainly losing more than she could afford. It would be a kindness to remove her from the table. It did not occur to Dolmain that he could always find an excuse to throw himself in the path of a charming lady.

"Come, let us dance," he said.

"I should love it of all things!" She scooped the few remaining counters up and handed them to Dolmain to put in his pocket. "I shall play again later," she said, and they walked away to the ballroom.

This was the really enjoyable part of the evening for her, and her eyes skimmed the room for eligible gentlemen. She was astonished to realize how many of them she had already tried to fall in love with, and failed. Lord Neville, too stodgy; Sir James Pyke, too rakish; Lord Anscombe, a wickedly engaging fortune hunter. The Season was amazingly thin of *partis*—and there would be so many pretty young debs in competition for them. As her eyes darted from dark head to brown to blond, she felt her enthusiasm dwindle. Really it was all becoming rather a bore. She remembered her first ball—it seemed aeons ago—when she had been so nervous. Now she was one of the blasé matrons. But Dolmain, at least, was interesting.

She turned to him and said, "I am a little surprised you came here tonight, Dolmain."

As he replied, his eyes raked her slowly from head to toe in the age-old way of a gentleman when he has found a lady who interests him. "I am mighty glad I did," he said.

She did not lower her eyes in maidenly modesty or blush at his bold assessment. She lifted her head and said flirtatiously, "And so am I, milord. Your pockets are deep. I hope you plan to dip into them for me." Now, why was he looking at her like that? "For my orphans, I mean," she added. "Shame on you, Lord Dolmain," she teased. "What were you thinking?" Had she imagined that glint of interest? Was it even remotely possible that Dolmain was on the lookout for a mistress?

"I was thinking you are a brass-faced minx, Lady Winbourne," he replied flirtatiously. "I had not realized you considered the orphans your own personal charge."

"I have long been interested in them."

Dolmain studied her every move. Despite his seldom running into Lady Winbourne, he was by no means unaware of her existence. He had envied

14

Julian his prize the first day he saw her and had followed her career with some interest. One marriage had been enough to satisfy him. Of course, a lord did require a son and heir. He must marry some worthy lady one day. In the meanwhile, there was nothing unusual in seeking the company of an obliging young widow to ease the pangs of lonesomeness. Whether Caro was obliging in that respect, he had yet to discover. Certainly no aroma of sanctity surrounded her. She was young; she was beautiful; presumably she missed her husband and was taking her pleasure where she found it—until she nabbed another husband. The trick would be to make sure he didn't end up in that role.

"Oh, good! A waltz!" she exclaimed, when the music began.

Dolmain welcomed the waltz, too. This new fad was the only thing that enabled a gentleman to publicly hold a lady in his arms without censure. Once the music began, he gathered her into his arms; they ceased talking and swirled about the floor in perfect harmony. She moved with the ease and grace of a fairy. Caroline was known as a marvelous dancer; she was surprised to see all her skills were required to keep pace with Dolmain.

She tilted her head back and gazed at him until he felt he was drowning in the depths of her long-lashed eyes. "Where did you learn to waltz like this?" she asked dreamily.

"At Whitehall," he replied soberly, but a lambent flicker of amusement flashed in his eyes as he said it. "Now that I have made my debut, however, I look forward to performing in public again soon—with you."

She drew her head back and cast a coquettish smile at him. "How nice. I expect we shall meet here and there."

"Very likely, but I prefer less happenstance in my dealings. Shall we say, tomorrow at four?"

"You have been out of it longer than you realize, Dolmain. Waltzes do not begin at four, unless you are suggesting we attend some deb's waltzing lessons."

"Nothing of the sort. You and I are well past the age where we require lessons. I meant we might go for a drive. It is difficult to hold any rational conversation at a place like this."

"I am not much good at rational discourse," she warned. "I leave that to you politicians. My forte is nonsense."

He lowered his head and whispered in her ear, "I shall let you in on all the naughty on-dits at Whitehall."

His lips tickled her ear, as he breathed into it. She gave an impish grin. "Is it true there is a war going on with some Frenchie—what is his name, now? Ah, Napoleon Bonaparte. That's it."

"And you told me your forte was nonsense. You are up to all the rigs. But seriously, Lady Winbourne, may I call tomorrow?"

"I would be honored," she said graciously. A spurt of triumph thrilled through her. Lord Dolmain would add a touch of class to her court of escorts. Yet she could not quite envisage him being content to be one of a throng.

When the waltzes were over, he accompanied her to the refreshment parlor. Due to the crowd, he walked a pace behind her. Warmed by the waltz, she let her shawl slip low over her shoulders, revealing the daring cut of her gown. Dolmain's eyebrows rose in surprise.

"Don't say it," she warned, with a saucy look tossed over her shoulder, for she suspected he would be shocked at her gown.

"I was not going to disparage it. How else could you show off that charming beauty mark? The gown is very nice, too."

"Thank you. Champagne for me, if you please. It

is an extravagance to serve it at a charity do, but it draws the better class. Orgeat is so old-fashioned," she said, with a *tsk* of disapproval.

"I assume, then, that you are a thoroughly modern lady?" he asked, and listened closely for her reply.

"I try to keep in the vanguard. I approve of all modern innovations—waltzing and Byron's poems and damped gowns."

"We think alike, you and I," he said approvingly.

"Then you, too, are ready to return to the roulette table," she said, when her glass was empty.

"Have another glass of wine first," he said, hoping to minimize her losses.

"Why, Dolmain, are you trying to get me intoxicated?"

"No, to keep you to myself a little longer."

She was flattered that he was enjoying her company, and had another glass. They flirted outrageously, each pleased with the other. The evening was not going as she expected, but it was enjoyable. After the second glass of wine, she insisted on returning to the gaming room, and Dolmain had no option but to return the counters he held for her.

He suggested she change her hundred-pound chips for ten-pound ones. "You gamble your way, I'll stick to my own. You must not try to change me, Lord Dolmain."

"Oh, come, now. You must allow me to *try*, at least."

As he played macao, he kept one eye on Caroline. He noticed that she was losing steadily, and seemed to be sad. He assumed she was regretting her losses, yet she kept on playing.

It was her memories of Julian that caused her wistfulness. She was bound to think of him on this special occasion. He was the one who had initiated gaming night, and now it had grown into this spectacular event. It seemed a fitting memorial to him.

17

How pleased he would have been to see his scandalous idea so successful—and how amused that it was now as respectable as the queen's drawing room. Three cabinet ministers were here. As the croupier raked her last counter off the board, she sighed with relief. Now she could go back to dancing.

Once away from the throng, she was ambushed by memories of other gaming nights, when she and Julian had gone out on the town after the last guest left, then gone home and made passionate love. She retired to a quiet alcove to think.

It was there that Dolmain found her. He had seen her leave the table, noticed her distraught air, and wondered just how much she had lost. She looked pale and sad.

"Let me take you home, Lady Winbourne," he said gently.

She looked up, startled to see him. Caught up in her memories, at his first appearance she had the absurd idea that he was Julian. "Yes, I would like to go home now," she said. The dancing she had been anticipating had lost its attraction. She would just go home to bed—and her memories of Julian.

"I came with Mr. Newton," she said. "I should tell him—"

"I shall tell him you are going home with me." Dolmain called for his carriage, then went to the faro table and gave Newton the message.

"What, Caro leaving before the last dog is hung?" Newt asked. "That ain't like her. Too much wine, I expect. Thankee, Dolmain. I have won a monkey. Wouldn't you know tonight I would win, when I have to stay until I lose it all again."

When Dolmain returned to her, he was solicitous of her comfort. He held her velvet wrap, and when he accompanied her to his carriage, he gave her his arm. In the shadowed carriage, he sat, not across from her, but on the banquette beside her.

"You seem sad, Lady Winbourne," he said, with some sympathy. "I hope you have not lost more than you can afford?"

"Oh no. It is not that," she assured him.

Of course, gamblers always denied their heavy losses. "Then what is troubling you?" he asked.

Dolmain didn't seem the kind of gentleman she could confide her innermost heart to. She shook herself out of her mood and replied, "I was just remembering my first Season. It seems so long ago."

"If it is any consolation, mine was a good deal longer ago than yours. You are still young, and very beautiful."

"Thank you," she said, placing her hand on his. "It is sweet of you to try to cheer me up, Dolmain. Actually, I was thinking of my husband. He loved our gaming night. But then, he enjoyed all of life, and made it enjoyable for others, too. Especially me," she added softly.

His hand closed comfortingly over hers. "It is hard to let go of the past, when the past was good," he said. "As you probably know, I am a widower myself."

"Yes, I know." It helped to have someone to share her memories with. Someone who understood, and felt as she felt.

"Life goes on, and we must go on with it. It is unhealthy to harp on the past. Let us try, if we can, to comfort each other."

"That would be nice," she said.

He drew her head onto his shoulder and put his arm around her, as the first step to embracing her more fully. He was somewhat surprised when she said in a trusting voice, "I never thought you would be so understanding, Dolmain. You always looked so toplofty, but you are very nice. I expect it was sorrow that made you look so severe."

"Severe! Is that how I looked to you? And here I

19

thought I was wearing a smile, at least when I went into company."

"You have got it all wrong. A smile turns the lips up." She playfully placed her fingers at the ends of his lips and drew them up. "Like that. You will soon get on to it."

He was about to pull her into his arms when she drew away. Tomorrow would be time enough to sound her out on what he had in mind. He knew Lady Winbourne had drunk a good deal of wine, and it would be ungentlemanly to take advantage of her. When he escorted her to the door of her house, he just kissed her lightly on the cheek, and said, "Sleep tight, milady."

Caroline went straight up to bed and fell asleep quickly, but awoke in the middle of the night with a sense of something left undone. What was it? She had said good night to Julian. But she had not told him about Dolmain. Was that it? She thought of Dolmain's unexpected kindness. Like her, he was lonesome. He must have been very much in love with his wife, to be still missing her after all these years. He seemed very nice. Perhaps she could help him forget. . . .

Chapter Three

Dolmain came the next afternoon at four, as agreed. On that fine spring afternoon, he was driving his open sporting carriage, a yellow curricle with shining silver appointments, drawn by a pair of blood grays. Caro knew at a glance that he cared more for his carriage and horses than for his toilette. His jacket was a fine piece of tailoring, but it was simply cut. His shirt points were low, and his cravat neither large nor intricate.

It was the custom for the ton to meet at the barrier at Hyde Park around four to gossip and discuss their evening plans. She expected they would go there, but when Dolmain suggested a drive out the Chelsea Road, she was happy to go along with it.

"As I sat in the House, looking out the window at the blue sky, I felt an urge to be in the country—with you," he said.

"Why me?"

"You are a little prettier than my groom," he replied blandly.

"Flattery will get you nowhere, Dolmain."

"Then I must think of some other ploy. I hope you have no objection to the open carriage?"

"I love it, especially in the country, with the wind in my hair. I shall take off my bonnet after we get out of town."

"Are you not afraid of freckles?" he asked, using it as an excuse to study her face. How youthful she looked, yet she was no green girl. She had been on the town for a decade.

"Not in the least. Why do you think God created rice powder?"

Once beyond city traffic, she removed her bonnet. The wind had its way with her raven curls, whipping them to and fro. It also brought a rosy flush to her ivory cheeks. The farms they drove by provided a subject for conversation. He was surprised to hear her speak knowledgeably of cows and corn and chickens. After they had driven five miles, she suggested they turn back.

"I thought we might stop at some small inn for tea," he said. In the more intimate atmosphere of a civilized private parlor, the romance would progress more quickly.

"Would an ale not be more enjoyable? I am feeling bucolic today, after seeing all those cows. We passed a small tavern on our way out of town. There it is, Jack Duck's Tavern."

He blinked in surprise. "But ladies don't go to places like that."

"I do. I depend on you to protect me."

"I doubt we will be physically attacked in broad daylight," he said uncertainly.

"Daylight is a sovereign prevention to be sure, but I only meant an attack on my fair name, if anyone should see us being so unstylish."

"Who will protect *my* reputation?"

"No one would dare to censure Lord Dolmain. You are above reproach. Something quite new for me, to have such an escort. What is the point of stepping out with such a top-of-the-trees gentleman if he cannot protect you from censure?"

"In that case, we may misbehave as much as we like, I take it?"

"Why, we may even throw caution to the winds and have two glasses of ale."

He admired her adroit manner of ignoring his

leading statements. Caro paid no heed to the sawdust on the floor and the plain deal table. When the innkeeper's dog strolled in and sat at her feet, she reached down and patted it.

"That dog has fleas," he warned her.

"Poor dog. Why don't they give him a bath with lye soap?"

"I see no evidence of soap ever being used in this place," Dolmain replied, casting an eye over the dim windows.

After two tankards of ale, Caro suggested they return to town. Dolmain was sorry the outing was over. He had enjoyed himself—but he had not gotten an inch closer to seducing her.

"Will you be at the ball this evening?" she asked, as they drove back.

No further identification of the party was necessary. "The ball" that evening was Lady Castlereagh's ball, the first large one of the new Season. It promised to be a glittering affair. Castlereagh was the foreign secretary, and his wife was one of the patronesses of Almack's, the most prestigious club in London. Dolmain's work brought him in frequent contact with Castlereagh, and despite the difference in their politics, they were friends. Dolmain had previously accepted an invitation to dine with the Castlereaghs before the ball, so Caro would go with Newt, as she had already arranged.

As she dressed for the do and had dinner with Georgie, she wondered what Dolmain was doing, and if he was thinking of her. Already he was becoming more than just a friend in her mind. He sent her a corsage of two white orchids. She was surprised at that streak of gallantry in him, and was touched that he had taken time out of his busy life to arrange for the flowers.

Newt arrived at the appointed hour, rumpled and inelegant as ever. "All set?" he asked.

"Ready to go."

"Where are we off to tonight?"

"Castlereaghs."

"Ah." A frown creased his brow as he rooted through his pockets, drawing out various crumpled invitations and pieces of paper and mumbling to himself, "Abercrombie's rout, a game of cards with Neill, Hoby—ten guineas for a new pair of boots." He crumpled the paper up and tossed it in the grate. "Not one sou for Hoby until he gets the squeak out of those boots. Castlereagh's seems to be the one card I left at home. I had one." He scratched his head, further destroying an already bad head of hair. "No matter. They'll let me in when I'm with you. Known to all the best butlers. Daresay you could walk in with Jack Ketch himself and no one would stop you."

"Let us go," Caro said, and waved good-bye to Georgie. She was so eager to see Dolmain again that she flew down the stairs and into the carriage. At the opening of the Season, the streets were alive with carriages. Lanterns blazed in front of the houses where a rout or ball was being held. The lineup of carriages in front of Castlereagh's was a block long. The younger guests, including Caro and Newt, deserted their carriages and walked to the door, leaving John Groom in charge of the horses.

Newt was admitted to the ball with no difficulty. They were soon standing in line, waiting to be announced. Caroline felt the tingling anticipation that always preceded a great ball, especially the first ball of the Season. The sensation was heightened on that occasion by her eagerness to be with Dolmain. She saw Lady Jersey and Emily Cowper. Of course they would be there, sister patronesses of Lady Castlereagh at Almack's. How the debs and their mamas would be scrambling to obtain vouchers. Without a voucher to Almack's, one might as well admit defeat and go back to the country. Only half a dozen of the three hundred officers of the Foot Guards had made it last year—younger sons of good and often noble families had been turned down.

Caro was a member. She was careful to attend a few assemblies each year to assure herself and society that she still belonged. Actually, the assemblies were an ordeal. Quadrilles and Scotch reels were the preferred dances, with only orgeat to slake the thirst. The playing of cards was allowed, but hardly more enjoyable, as the play was for chicken stakes.

Caroline's eyes skimmed the room, looking for Dolmain. Her heart raced when she spotted his dark head amidst the throng on the dance floor. The opening minuet was already in progress. Her next interest was to see who he was dancing with. She felt a definite lurch of jealousy when she saw his companion, a young lady in white—a deb. It was not just that he was standing up with her, but the intimate way he smiled at her. Surely he was well past the age for debutantes. It seemed he had a colt's tooth in his head. The girl was a pretty blonde, but young enough to be his daughter.

Caroline had the first set with Newton. Her major preoccupation was to keep away from his marauding toes; his was to spy out the new batch of young ladies making their curtseys.

"The one with the yaller curls," he said, as the dance drew to a close. "Can you present me to her, Caro?"

"Which one?"

"By the living jingo, she is coming toward us." He twitched at his jacket. "Daresay I look like an unmade bed."

Caroline looked around and saw Lord Dolmain coming in her direction, accompanied by the young lady he had been dancing with when they arrived. She felt a little surge of triumph.

25

"Lady Winbourne," he said, with one of his businesslike bows, but his eyes spoke a more intimate story as they gazed into hers. "I would like you to meet my daughter, Lady Helen. She is making her debut this year."

"Your daughter!" Relief and surprise mingled inside her. "Good gracious, you cannot mean your daughter is making her bows."

As she turned immediately to greet Lady Helen and present Mr. Newton, she failed to observe the flash of embarrassment that Dolmain was suffering. He felt like an imposter. He hadn't told Caro Helen's age.

Caro assessed the girl's appearance and demeanor as she made the introduction. She was pretty and well behaved. Very well turned out, too, in a properly modest white gown, but those garish diamonds! They did not belong on a deb. They looked more like the bounty worn by the muslin company. Why had he allowed his daughter to wear them?

Newt wasted no time in detaching Lady Helen for the next set.

"My secret is out," Dolmain said, as his daughter left. "You may call me Lord Methuselah."

"Why did you not tell me she is making her debut?"

"Because it makes me feel ancient."

"Nonsense! She is very pretty, Dolmain. She does you proud. She must take after her mama."

"Do I detect the aroma of insult in there?" he asked, smiling.

She waggled a playful finger at him. "Sunk to fishing for compliments, Dolmain? That was not my meaning. I am referring to her coloring and her general getup. She does not take after you. I never met Lady Dolmain."

"No, she was gone before you hit London."

"You make me sound like a tornado! So it is Lady

26

Helen's debut that accounts for your foray into society this year. I wondered, when I first saw you at the gaming hell, what had pried you loose from Whitehall."

"Now you are making *me* sound like a barnacle. You must know a papa's work is never done." He turned to gaze at his daughter, who was talking to Newton across the room.

"Yours soon will be, Dolmain. She is very fetching. You will have no trouble getting her bounced off. Do you have other children you have been hiding from me?" she asked, with a teasing smile.

"Just the one, and to tell the truth, I am in no hurry to lose her. She has reached the ripe old age of seventeen, however, and her aunt, Lady Milchamp, tells me it is time to place her on the Marriage Mart, before she fancies herself in love with some uncouth country lad. Aunt Milchamp has volunteered to undertake chaperoning duties for the Season, but for the first ball, I wanted to tag along."

"It seems impossible your daughter is making her debut, Dolmain. You must have married very young."

"Killed in covert, ma'am. A stripling of twenty years. To save you the bother of doing the arithmetic, I am eight and thirty years old. And you, if memory serves, must be—"

"There is no need to go into that, sir."

A smile tugged at his lips. "Vain creature. In any case, you do not *look* twenty-seven."

"You are too horrid. Is a lady allowed no secrets?"

"Surely a lady's life is an open book. She has no need of secrets."

She lifted a well-arched eyebrow in derision. "What a dead bore she would be without them. We all have our little secret vices, you must know."

"And yours is an unreasonable fear of arithmetic. Let us speak of other things. I see you are wearing

27

the orchids. My uncle breeds them. That one is called the Incomparable, which is why I wanted you to have it."

"A very pretty compliment, sir."

The cotillion began and they took their place in the set with Helen and Newt and the other couples. When the set was finished, they went to the refreshment parlor. Dolmain procured wine for them and they moved to the edge of the room to talk. Several guests who remembered how the gaming night had begun congratulated Caroline on its continued success. She explained to Dolmain that it had been her late husband's idea.

"I believe I remember it now. The first few years it was held at Winbourne House, if memory serves. A little risqué—like that gown you wore the other night."

"You said you liked it," she reminded him.

"I did. It suited you."

"Are you calling me risqué? I take leave to tell you, any gentleman who would allow his young daughter to make her bows wearing a set of diamonds more suitable to a lightskirt is no judge of ladies' fashion."

"A lightskirt! The necklace may be vulgar, but it is not the sort of present a man gives a lightskirt—unless he is a fool. It is worth thirty thousand pounds."

"That much! What a waste of blunt. I could put the money to better use." She thought of what could be done for the orphans with that sum.

"I oughtn't to have let Helen wear them," he admitted. "The diamonds belonged to her mama. She particularly wanted to wear them this evening. Helen is a very well-behaved girl as a rule, but headstrong. She is studious and full of good works, but undeniably headstrong. We did mention she takes after her mama," he added with a grin. "If you could talk her into putting them in her reticule, I would be eternally grateful."

"I doubt she would listen to me."

"Now, there you are mistaken, ma'am. She most particularly admired your toilette. I think you might hint her into a more proper style, if you cared to."

"My risqué style, you mean?"

He looked at her with the ghost of a smile touching his lips. "That would not suit my daughter. I meant your other style, the country girl I caught a glimpse of this afternoon."

Caroline sensed that he was mentally sizing her up for the role of Helen's stepmama. It was too early for this, but she liked Dolmain and was willing to take an interest in the girl. She had no notion of giving advice so early in the acquaintance, however. If, in future, they became friends, then she would drop Helen a gentle hint.

After they had drunk their wine, Caroline went to tidy her hair in the ladies' parlor. The room, like the ball, was a squeeze. Helen was there, as was Lady Milchamp. Helen sat in a corner apart from the others. Caroline noticed she was wearing only one slipper. She went to have a word with the girl.

"What happened to your slipper?" she asked.

"Mr. Newton broke the buckle on it. A servant is having it repaired or replaced."

"Oh dear. I am sorry. Newt is not much of a dancer."

"We were not dancing. We were just standing there talking when Mr. Newton tripped over the rug. He was not even walking at the time. I cannot imagine how it happened. He spilt his wine, too. Fortunately not on me."

"That was good luck. It would have made a mess of a white gown." Poor Newt. Another lady displeased with him before he even got to know her.

Helen opened her reticule and took out her comb.

She wore her hair pulled back from her face, fastened at the back with a jeweled comb, which had become loose from dancing. As she fumbled with the hair clasp, Caro offered to help her. She bent over and unfastened it, then combed the hair back smoothly and fastened it again.

"There, that is better," she said.

"Thank you, Lady Winbourne."

Caroline glanced at the large, unsuitable necklace, but decided it would offend Lady Helen if she said anything. She left in search of Newt. Perhaps a servant could do something with his jacket. She met Newt hovering in the corridor beyond the ballroom.

"Oh dear!" she exclaimed, when she saw his cravat and shirtfront all blotched with red wine.

"Wouldn't you know, I came out without a handkerchief," he said, shaking his brindled head.

She rooted in her reticule and gave him hers. "A bit of water might remove the stain."

"I'll try it, but sometimes I find it doesn't always work." One of Newt's distinctions was his making a fricassee of the king's English. He took the handkerchief and wandered off in search of water.

Dolmain watched the interlude from across the room. He was still watching a little later when his daughter came out of the ladies' parlor, without her diamonds. A small smile tugged at his lips. So the redoubtable Lady Winbourne had talked Helen into removing the garish necklace! He assumed the necklace was wrapped in the handkerchief she had entrusted to Newton.

He expected Newton was even then looking for him to return it. Unfortunately, he could not go after Newton. Castlereagh wanted to have a private coze with him in his study about the shipment of supplies to Wellington in the Peninsula. Castlereagh had learned that the last shipment did not reach Spain. Whether it had been sabotage or accident was not yet clear, but they had to discuss safeguards for the next shipment. He had no fears for the necklace's safety. Caro knew how valuable it was and would see it was kept safe. He would pick it up when he called on her tomorrow afternoon. He had already given a footman a note to give Caro, explaining his absence from the remainder of the ball and asking permission to call on her the next day at four.

Newton managed to make such a mess of his shirt and cravat that he had to go home to change. When Caro received Dolmain's note, she decided to leave, too. She had no interest in anyone else. She had Newt drop her off at Berkeley Square, where she discussed the ball with Georgie over a cup of cocoa, then went to bed early.

She didn't think of the necklace again until the next morning when Dolmain came to call.

Chapter Four

Caroline was at breakfast at eight-thirty the next morning. Both the early hour and her modest serge suit were a surprise to her servants. Once the Season began, milady often slept late, and usually dressed in the highest kick of fashion. The plain suit was in honor of the ladies from the Orphans' Fair Day committee (some of them high sticklers), who were meeting that day at Berkeley Square. A part of the proceeds from the gaming night went to sponsor a holiday in the country for the orphans. There would be contests, races, all sorts of games, and prizes and refreshments to be arranged.

She was surprised to hear the door knocker sound at eight-thirty, and simply astonished to hear Lord Dolmain's accents. What could he want? Crumm knew she was up, so she waited for him to show Dolmain in.

"A tall drink of water has stopped to see you," Crumm said. "I told him you was up and about. He is there now, burning a hole in the carpet." He handed her Dolmain's card.

"Show him in, Crumm," she said, smiling.

Dolmain wore a distracted expression when he duly appeared at the door. He performed one of his curt bows. Caroline's smile faded. She said, "Good morning, Dolmain," in a questioning way, and invited him to take a cup of coffee.

"I expect you know why I am here," he said, sitting down. Like her servants, he was surprised to find her up and about so early. He did not notice her suit. His attention was riveted on her violet eyes and dewy skin. Sunlight slanting through the window behind her cast shimmering lights of rose and amber and peacock blue on her raven hair.

"I hope you have not come to cancel our drive!" she exclaimed, with a pout of disappointment.

"Not at all. I look forward to our outing. I have come to collect Helen's necklace."

She stared at him, a frown puckering her brow, and asked, "What on earth are you talking about, Dolmain?"

His smile faded, and his face froze into a mask of incomprehension. "You do have her necklace, do you not?"

"The one she wore last night? No, why should I have it?"

"But she was not wearing it when she left the ladies' room last night. You came out just before her. We had discussed your talking her out of wearing it. I made sure it was the necklace I saw you hand to Newton."

"No! It was only a handkerchief. He spilled wine on his cravat." She felt a jolt of something unpleasant. "Are you saying the necklace is missing?"

"Lady Milchamp was waiting for me when I returned last night. She said Helen's necklace was missing. I assumed you had it."

"Did Helen say so?" she demanded. The vaguely unpleasant sensation was quickly rising to anger.

"No, Helen did not mention it at all. I can only assume she did not notice it was gone, nor apparently did Lady Milchamp, at first. It was half an hour after Helen was in bed that Lady Milchamp decided the thing ought to be put in the safe. She went to get it, and it was not in Helen's room. She spoke to her dresser, who claimed she had not seen it. The dresser did not know Helen was wearing the diamonds. I gave them to her after she came down-

33

stairs last night, already dressed, so that is not surprising. Lady Milchamp was concerned enough
that she looked in Helen's reticule and in her pockets. The necklace was not there. She was about to
awaken her and ask her about it when I returned.
I told her I thought you had it. She was greatly relieved, but as she had not seen Helen give it to you,
I decided to stop and just check that you did have
it. It is very valuable."

"Thirty thousand pounds," Caro said, in a frightened whisper. "You must get on to Lady Castlereagh at once, Dolmain! The clasp must have
broken, and the necklace fallen off unnoticed.
Helen was sitting on that settee in the corner when
I was in the ladies' parlor. She was wearing the diamonds then. I remember thinking it was not a
good time to mention them, when she was a trifle
miffed with Newton for having broken her shoe
buckle. Perhaps the necklace has got pushed under
the sofa, or down the side of the cushioned seat."

Dolmain rubbed his neck, frowning. "Yes, that
must be what happened. I shall drop by there before I go to Whitehall."

"Or perhaps you should go home and speak to
Helen first. Might she have given the necklace to
someone to hold for her if the clasp broke?"

"I should think she would have given it to Lady
Milchamp, but perhaps if she was dancing with
some gentleman she knew and trusted . . . Yes, you
are right. I must speak to Helen before making a
fuss."

"I do hope this is all a tempest in a teapot," Caroline said, frowning. "So vexing for Lady Castlereagh if the necklace is missing and does not turn
up. Why, it would mean someone had stolen it."

Dolmain's dark eyes opened a shade wider in
alarm. He rose, saying, "I must go at once."

"You will let me know what you learn?"

"Yes, I shall drop a note if I am unable to keep our date."

Caroline had hoped to hear the outcome before four o'clock, but she could see Dolmain was anxious and did not wish to further hamper his activities. She had poured him a cup of coffee when he came in, but he had not touched it.

"I hope everything turns out well," she said.

"I am sure the thing is about somewhere. Pray, do not trouble yourself about it." He bowed and left.

She sat on alone, thinking about last night. Helen had definitely been wearing the necklace when last she saw her. If she was not wearing it when she left the ladies' room, then it had either fallen off and was in the room, or she had given it to someone to hold. Or worst of all, some light-fingered lady had pocketed it. This, she was very reluctant to believe.

She discussed the matter with Georgie when her sister-in-law joined her for breakfast.

"That would be the famous Dolmain diamond necklace, that old Lord Dolmain gave his bride as a wedding gift in the last century," Georgiana said. "A great ugly thing, but very valuable, of course. I wondered that the present lord's wife did not have it refashioned. But then, she liked those gaudy pieces of jewelry. A foreigner," she said dismissingly.

"A foreigner? I did not know that."

"She was French." The lady's tight lips suggested this was the worst sort of foreigner. "One of the émigrés who escaped during the revolution in France. She landed at Brighton Beach on a little boat set down from a frigate. She had been rescued from a raft in the Channel, folks said. She was monstrously pretty—a petite blonde. Prinny and his set took her up. Dolmain met her in Brighton, and fell in love at sight. A pity, really. He was so

35

young. She was not slow to get a ring around her finger. Married him up on the sly in Brighton, and presented old Lord Dolmain with a fait accompli."

"I cannot imagine Dolmain doing anything so dashing," Caroline said, blinking in astonishment.

"Oh, he was a wild colt in those days. They do say that wild colts make the best horses when they mature, and it seems to be the case with Dolmain. It was after he came back from France that he settled down and became a force in politics."

"What was he doing in France?"

"He was sent over as a secretary to run errands during the signing of the Peace of Amiens in 1802. You would not remember it, but we actually signed a peace treaty with that Corsican rascal at one time. I expect Dolmain's wife egged him on to get the assignment as secretary. She never did settle into our English ways. There were many who felt it was no loss when she did not return with him."

Caroline stared. This story went from strange to downright incredible. When she spoke, her voice was high with disbelief. "You cannot mean she *left* him! Are you saying he has a wife?"

"Oh no, she did die eventually, but she never returned from France at all. I never heard what happened. It was all kept very hush-hush. There was all manner of rumor, of course. Some said she was involved in spying for England, some hinted she was working for the other side. The official version was that she stayed in France to try to reclaim her family's estate. In any case, she never came back."

"When did she die?"

"I really have no idea, Caro, but she must have died, for there was never any talk of divorce, and Dolmain offered for Lady Mary Swann five years ago."

"I remember he was seeing her. I had not heard it came to an offer." The idea occurred to her that

36

Dolmain was altar-shy. Was he still in love with his late wife?

"Oh, she would have had him fast enough, but her papa had rigged up some match with a cousin, and she went along with it. Old Swann was a bear for having his own way."

Caroline just sat, trying to digest all this. Her only objection to Dolmain was that, after Julian, he might seem a trifle serious for her taste. He certainly took his work more seriously than Julian had ever done. To hear of his youthful exploits lent him an air of recklessness that made him irresistible.

"It is hard to believe any of Lady Castlereagh's guests would have stolen the necklace," Georgiana said. "I wonder if she hired extra servants for the ball. If one of them got away with it, Dolmain can hardly hope to recover it. It is odd that neither Lady Helen nor Lady Milchamp noticed it was missing."

"Indeed it is. The first time I wore the diamonds Julian gave me, I thought of nothing else all evening. One's first diamonds are like a first kiss."

Georgie gave a sigh. She would not know about that. She felt a sting of resentment to consider how all romance was missing from her life. "Pity," she said, then turned the discussion to the meeting to plan the orphans' holiday.

Caroline pushed the affair to the back of her mind, but could not entirely forget it. While the ladies met and talked, one corner of her mind kept waiting to hear the door knocker, heralding Dolmain's visit. The meeting broke up at three, which gave her time to arrange a more interesting toilette for her drive with Dolmain, as he had not written to cancel it.

He came at four, as planned. She knew as soon as she saw his haggard face that he had not found the diamonds. Her heart went out to him in his trouble.

"What did Lady Helen have to say?" she asked.

"She has absolutely no notion what could have happened to the diamonds," he said grimly. "She did not know they were missing until I had her awoken after I left you this morning and asked her about them. Apparently she never gave them a thought when she was undressing. She was fagged from the ball, she said. I called on Lady Castlereagh. We searched every square inch of the parlor the ladies used last night. She called her servants and questioned them. No one saw the necklace."

"Did she hire extra servants for the ball?"

"No, she had her own servants from Cray's Foot come up to town for the party. She trusts them implicitly. There was only one servant in the ladies' parlor, a Miss Henshaw, whom she has known forever. After meeting Henshaw, I am convinced of her innocence."

"Then some lady has pocketed them," Caroline said reluctantly. "How vexing for Lady Castlereagh. I know how she must feel. Timmy Fellows once lost a ruby cravat pin at Winbourne House. I felt it was my fault, although I had not even noticed the thing. Julian insisted on buying him a replacement."

"I shan't let Castlereagh do that."

They sat a moment. It was obvious that Dolmain was in no mood to go for their drive.

"Did you search the carriage?" she asked him.

"I did, but I already knew the necklace was not there. She wore it into that parlor, and came out without it, after speaking to you."

Again Caroline felt that sting of something unpleasant. "I hope you are not suggesting that I took it!" she said, her voice rising perceptibly.

She watched as he raised his dark eyes and gazed at her, with a questioning look. "No, of course not," he said, but his tone lacked conviction.

"That *is* what you think," she said, in a voice of mingled anger, horror, and disbelief. "You think I stole the ugly thing!"

"Of course I don't," he shot back. "But it is odd we were speaking of it just before it vanished. You recall I mentioned its value, and you said you could put the money to better use. Lady Milchamp and Helen both mentioned that you made a point of speaking to Helen. You were with her on the sofa for a moment, I think, helping her with her corsage or some such thing."

"I helped her arrange her hair. I never touched the necklace. I am not a magician, after all, that I could induce it to fly into my pocket without touching it."

"It seems someone did," he shot back. Then he hastily added, "No one is accusing you, however."

"You are not far from it, with those insinuating remarks."

"Miss Henshaw was watching you particularly. She mentioned you kept your back to her; your body was between Helen and the rest of the room. She didn't notice whether Helen was still wearing the necklace when you left. Then you left the ball very soon after leaving the ladies' parlor."

The thing went from bad to worse. "So did you leave it!" she shot back. "But are you saying you quizzed Lady Castlereagh's servants about me, in particular? That you singled *me* out for special investigation? Is that what you are saying?"

"Not you in particular. I merely asked her if she had noticed who Helen spoke to. She mentioned you—and no one else."

"Good God! You might as well have sent Bow Street to search my house. You know how servants tattle. The story will be all over town by morning. How could you do such a thing, Lord Dolmain?"

Dolmain, in his concern for the necklace, had not viewed the matter in this light, but as he listened, he realized he might inadvertently have cast a shadow on Lady Winbourne's reputation. His chagrin was not so great as it might have been, however, as he still harbored a lingering suspicion that Caroline had taken the diamonds. She did not have the reputation of a thief, but she was known as a dashing lady who lived exceedingly well for a dowager. Julian's estate had gone to young Jeremy Eden. It was not an enormously wealthy estate, yet the widow did not bother to live in the Dower House. She had her own place in Kent, along with this mansion in London. And most damning of all was her love of gambling, and her unlucky way with the dice.

"I shall make it clear to society that you are not involved," he said stiffly.

"Thank you very much. Very kind of you, when you have already cast suspicion on me. Naturally I have every confidence in your discretion," she retorted. "Society will soon make clear there is no smoke without fire. Upon my word, I think you have behaved very badly in this affair."

An angry hue suffused his cheeks. He deeply regretted his rash behavior. If Caroline was innocent, and really he did not think she had taken the demmed thing, then he must do something for her. "The matter will be rectified," he said. "Will you do me the honor of attending Lady Brockley's ball this evening, ma'am?"

"No, I will not, thank you very much."

"If you are concerned for your reputation, then the rumors will soon die down if we are seen to be on the best of terms. That should prove to society that I do not suspect you."

She rose imperiously. "I do not require your protection, sir. I am not on probation. I would as lief go out with Jack Ketch. You may leave now, milord."

Dolmain rose slowly, wondering how he ought to handle this touchy situation. As the lady was so hot at hand, it was clear that he must keep his head. "I think you would be wise to do as I say, Lady Winbourne.

"We have already squeezed that lemon."

"A reputation, once lost, is not easily recovered," he cautioned.

Her nostrils flared dangerously. "You would be wise to leave before I call Crumm," she said through clenched teeth.

"I think I could take Crumm, should the need arise. If you refuse to be reasonable, I don't see what else I can do."

Her violet eyes were dark with violence. "You have done quite enough. Good day."

"As you wish, milady."

He bowed and strolled out with an air of ease he was far from feeling.

Caroline was still in the boughs when Alfred Newton was shown in later. "You must take me to Brockley's ball tonight, Newt," she said. "Everyone thinks I have stolen Lady Helen's diamond necklace."

"Who says so?" Newt demanded. He could turn quite fierce when those he loved were wronged.

She outlined her visit with Dolmain. "Thing to do, we'll get our heads together," he said. "Two heads are better than none."

"I must definitely attend the ball. To stay away would be tantamount to declaring myself guilty."

"Absolutely. Besides, if someone is stabbing you in the back, you want to be there. The fact is, Dolmain hasn't a case to stand on. You wasn't the only one in the room with Lady Helen. The fellow must be tuppence shy of a shilling to say such a thing. Perfect rubbish."

But it was the sort of rubbish that could ruin a lady's reputation.

Chapter Five

She would go to Lady Brockley's ball with her faithful friend, Newton, and stare down anyone who dared to look at her askance. She wore a demure white gown from her first Season to emphasize her innocence, and at her throat the diamond-and-amethyst necklace that Julian had bought her to match her eyes.

Caroline was aware, as soon as she entered the room, that she had become an object of high curiosity. She was accustomed to attention but not this much, and not of this sort. Questioning eyes peered at her obliquely. Voices whispered behind raised fans. Heads had a way of turning from her as she advanced. The usual crush of black jackets did not rush forth to greet her. She was not lacking for partners, but they were not partners off the top shelf as she was accustomed to.

She pretended to ignore it, but she felt a gathering heaviness inside her to realize that her friends thought she was a thief. And it was Dolmain who had made them think it. That injustice burned like a coal in her heart. She refused to be browbeaten into submission. She danced and laughed merrily to show her unconcern. It would be all right. When Dolmain came, she would have to stand up with him. That would show the old cats they were wrong. But by eleven o'clock, Dolmain had still not come and she could take it no more.

When Newton appeared at her side, she was ready to leave.

"What do you say we go home now, Newt?" she suggested.

"All the same to me. Half of one, six dozen of t'other. Or better, let us shag off to the Pantheon. It might raise a few eyeballs, but that never bothers you." She had been nagging him to take her last year. Not the thing, really. Lightskirts and worse, but the racier members of the ton went as well. Caro needed something to buck up her spirits.

Caroline felt it might do her good to round out the evening amongst less demanding company. The idea of wearing a mask appealed to her. People would not recognize her and stare.

"We'll have to go home to pick up masks and dominoes."

Once at the Pantheon, Caroline was disappointed to see it was not the disreputable den she had been imagining. Georgie had told her that when it opened forty-odd years ago, it had been *the* place for the ton to go. Julian's parents had been amongst the seventeen hundred attending the opening assembly.

Inside, it was decorated in the Italian style, with frescoes on walls and ceilings. The lamps were hidden in antique vases, giving a soft, diffused illumination. Some of them hung on gilt chains from the ceiling, and some were atop marble pillars. Marble statues of Romans looked down from their lofty perch. It was like a grand mansion. If the crowd was from the demimonde, their dominoes and masks concealed the fact.

"What a take-in!" she exclaimed. "I expected a den of vice, and find a fancy ballroom."

"I don't understand why well-bred ladies always want to go throwing themselves into vice dens," Newt grouched. "Since we are here, might as well wet our whistles, eh?"

He led her to a box in the upper gallery that gave

a view of the dancers below, and ordered a bottle of wine. From this height, Caroline could see that the behavior was not so polite as she had thought. The music was a waltz, causing a wince of memory of her waltz with Dolmain. He thought no more of her than those trollops below. The dancers did not keep the proper distance between them by any means. Some of the gentlemen danced with both arms around their ladies, often swooping off into corners to embrace quiet licentiously.

Most of the gentlemen wore black dominoes and masks, but some of the females wore colors. Upon examining the women, Caroline was surprised to recognize a few of her own friends amongst the throng. Surely that was Miss Tallman in the red domino, and her fiancé with her. A bishop's daughter, imagine! She recognized a few others as well. One elegant blonde in a blue domino caught her attention. Had she not seen that lady at some ton party last night? The hair was arranged in a familiar manner, drawn back from the face into a bundle of curls.

"Good God! That is Lady Helen!" she exclaimed.

"Eh?"

"The blue domino on the left side of the floor."

Newt peered down. "I believe you're right. Shockin'!"

"Who is she with? It cannot be Dolmain!"

"No, the man ain't tall enough. I don't recognize the lad."

"You must find out who he is, Newt. I wager Dolmain has no idea his daughter is here. What a bold baggage she is. I feel guilty for being here, and I am a decade older than Lady Helen, and a widow besides."

"How would I find out?" he asked.

"We shall wait until the dance finishes and see which box they go to."

They both watched Helen and her partner. The

couple did not behave in any licentious manner. The gentleman held her a respectful two inches from him at all times. Lady Helen had obviously been taking waltzing lessons, and equally obviously, one of the two required more lessons before waltzing in public. They often stopped, indicating a misstep on someone's part. When she figured the dance was nearly over, Caro asked Newt to go belowstairs to follow them.

He was gone an unconscionably long time. Long enough for two separate gents to try their hand at joining Caroline. She had a little difficulty dispatching the second man, until she spotted Mr. Talon, a friend, passing in the corridor, and called for his assistance.

Mr. Talon returned after he had ejected the unwanted guest. "Surely you are not alone here, Caro?" he asked.

"I am with Mr. Newton. He will be back presently."

"I shall stay with you until he comes. Do you think this a wise time for you to be here?"

"What do you mean?" she asked, but she had a sinking feeling that she knew.

"With the Dolmain necklace business hanging over your head. Of course, we all know you did not take it," he assured her, "but it might be wise to stick to the straight and narrow for a few weeks. Chapel Royal on Sunday, concerts of antique music—just until the necklace turns up."

"Where did you hear about it?" she asked.

"At St. James's. The odds are five to one you are innocent, if that makes you feel better."

"I see the gentlemen are more lenient than the ladies," she said with a *tsk* of annoyance. Now she was a subject of gossip at the men's clubs. Was there no end to her shame?

"The cats have been cutting you, have they?"

"Not the cut direct. Let us say they have been avoiding me."

"I hope you know you can always count on me."

"Thank you, Mr. Talon. I appreciate it."

Newt soon returned. Caroline thanked Mr. Talon and saw him out of the box before quizzing Newton. "Did you discover who she is with?" she asked him.

"I loitered outside their box, pretending I was waiting for someone. They left the door open. They all took their masks off except Lady Helen, once they were in their box. There was an older, respectable-looking lady with them. Not Lady Milchamp. I did not recognize the dame. Dark hair with a bit of gray on the sides. A sharp-faced lady, but not actually hatchet-faced. The chit called her Mam'selle Blanchard. The lad was a handsome rogue, a Frenchie. She called him Bernard. There was another couple as well. A good-looking lady they called Renée, and a gray-haired gent with her. Foreigners, the lot of them, except for Helen. They was all parlaying the bongjaw."

"French? I wonder who they could be."

"That is as much as I could discover."

"You have done well. How on earth did Lady Helen escape her chaperon? You may be sure Dolmain has no idea she is here. Let us follow them when they leave and make sure she gets home safely."

"She ain't wearing any diamonds, if that is what concerns you."

Caroline blinked. "Are you hinting that this Bernard fellow is the thief? What an interesting idea!"

"Except he wasn't at Castlereagh's last night. Never saw him before. Pity they was all rattling off the bongjaw. I could not make heads or tails of what they was saying."

"Helen's mama was French," Caroline said, wondering if this was of any importance. How could it

47

be? The lady had been dead for over five years. And as she had left England in 1802, when Helen was only seven years old, the girl would have very little recollection of her mama. No, this was all irrelevant. The necklace had disappeared in Lady Castlereagh's parlor last night.

"Let us have your carriage called and wait outside to follow Lady Helen when she comes out," Caro suggested.

"Sure you have had your fill of low life? Mean to say, you have not had a jig yet."

"Another time. This is more important."

"Just as you wish," Newt said. He took an uninterested look around and said, "A dandy place." Then he finished off one glass of wine, looked unhappily at the nearly full bottle, and rose.

He had his carriage called and ordered his groom to wait half a block down Oxford Street, ready to follow when he gave the signal. It was not long before a blue domino came out, accompanied by Bernard but no chaperon.

"That's them right enough," Newt said, and gave the drawstring a jerk to signal his groom to follow the carriage.

"Imagine the chaperon letting that child go unaccompanied in a carriage with a strange man," Caro scolded. Despite her disgust with Dolmain, she could not let his innocent young daughter fall into the hands of some roué. After her experience with Dolmain, her sentiments were all on the side of innocent ladies.

"We don't know he's strange," Newt pointed out. "Mean to say, he might be a cousin for all we know."

"That is true, but we shall keep close behind them. If he tries to spirit her off—"

Newt reached into the side pocket and drew out a pistol. "I always come prepared," he said.

"An excellent idea. Julian told me I should always keep a pistol in the carriage."

It was almost a letdown when the carriage proceeded at a stately pace directly toward Lord Dolmain's mansion on Curzon Street. It stopped half a block away, however. Newt's groom pulled to a stop at the corner. They waited for five minutes, the tension mounting higher by the moment. Caro was struck with awful images of the poor girl struggling with an amorous man.

"I am going to see what is happening," she declared, and opened the door.

Just as she alit, the other carriage door opened and the man assisted Helen from the rig. Caro was overcome with curiosity. She wanted to learn what was passing between the two. She scanned the dark street, and thought she might approach Dolmain's house without being seen in her dark domino. She would not walk on the street, but stay close to the two intervening houses. By running, she reached the house next door to Dolmain's before Helen and her companion. A stand of tall yews grew in front of the house. She darted behind it, just at the outer edge of the house, and listened.

The conversation between Lady Helen and her friend was by no means amorous. "You are sure she is all right?" Helen asked in a worried voice. She spoke French, but Caro caught the gist of it. "She can come to London, now that she has the money?"

"She will be here soon."

"How soon? When can I expect her?"

"Very soon. We shall be in touch. You must go now. Be brave, *ma petite.*" He squeezed her fingers and left. Caroline waited, wondering if the girl would go into the house alone. How would she explain herself to the butler? The girl took a key out of her purse, unlocked the door, and walked in.

Nothing further could be learned, so Caroline hurried back to Newt's carriage.

"Where the deuce was you?" Newt asked. "I was half of a mind to go after you."

"I was eavesdropping. Let us follow Bernard."

Newt pulled the drawstring, but when they turned the corner in pursuit of Bernard, two similar carriages were on the road in front of them. One of them turned at the next corner. They followed it for a block; it stopped, and a party of four got out and went into a house.

"We've lost him," Newt said. "Pity. Shall we take a run back to the Pantheon and see if Blanchard and the others are still there?"

"No, I think not. I am more interested in Bernard." She told Newt what she had overheard as they drove to Berkeley Square. Newt went in for a drink and to discuss what they should do.

"Lady Helen said, 'Now that she has the money.' I wonder what she meant by that," Caroline said.

"And who 'she' is," Newt added, tugging at his ear.

"It could be anyone."

"I daresay it is."

"It must be someone she is very eager to see in London, though."

"A friend or cousin," Newt suggested. "Lady Helen must have sent blunt to someone. Kind of her."

"Yes, if that is what is going on."

"No mention of the necklace?"

"Not a word. She seems remarkably unconcerned for a young lady who has just misplaced a necklace worth a fortune."

An idea was scratching at the back of Caroline's mind. It was so devious, she hardly liked to express it, but she had to wonder if the money Helen spoke of had come from selling the necklace. That would mean Lady Helen had hidden the necklace and only claimed it had been lost or stolen to get the money without Dolmain becoming suspicious. But would the girl give so much money only to assure the company of a friend or cousin? No, she must be mistaken. Besides, the necklace could hardly have been sold so quickly. It had only gone missing the night before.

The whole affair was very odd. Caroline was extremely loath to call on Dolmain. She would rather have a tooth drawn than speak to him, but she felt it her duty to inform him that his daughter had been at the disreputable Pantheon, and come home alone in a carriage with a man. She also disliked to tattle on the girl, but if Helen were her daughter, she would expect her friends to do no less. Bernard might be anyone, a gazetted flirt, a fortune hunter, a rakehell.

She decided she would write to Dolmain rather than call on him. Helen was safe at home, so she would write her note tonight and have it dispatched early in the morning, to ensure Dolmain's receiving it before he went to the House.

"A taking little thing, Lady Helen, ain't she?" Newt said, with a moonish look on his face that revealed he was once more on the trail of a wife. "A mile above me, of course. I could not hope to win her with a ten-foot pole."

"She is a minx. I do not trust her above half."

"I like those green eyes," Newt continued. "Not cat eyes. I don't care for a cat's eye in a lady's face. More like a dog's eye really. Friendly. I wonder if she would like to go for a drive tomorrow."

Caro did not think there was much danger of Lady Helen accepting the offer. She had seemed quiet vexed with Newt for destroying the buckle of her slipper the evening before.

"You can ask her," she said with a shrug.

"P'raps I will. Well, I am off. I'll keep my ear to the ground. Bernard. I wonder if that is his first or last name. I know a Bernard Tyson, and a George Bernard. Odd, that."

"Do let me know if you discover anything."

Newt finally left, and Caroline wrote her note to be delivered to Dolmain early in the morning. She left the note with Crumm, then went to bed, where she tossed and turned for an hour before falling into a fitful sleep.

Chapter Six

Caroline looked so pale the next morning after her poor night's sleep that she resorted to the rouge pot before going downstairs. She felt certain Dolmain would call in person, and did not want him to see how much he had hurt her. She chose a gold-and-green striped lutestring walking dress in the latest jet of fashion to give her confidence. She would behave with cool civility, and when he left, she would not spend her day hiding her head and repining as if she were guilty, but would go on the strut on New Bond Street.

The rouge gave her a touch of color, but nothing could give her an appetite. She did not even lift the lids of the hot dishes on the sideboard, but accepted a cup of coffee and sat, sipping it, waiting for Dolmain to come. Her note to him had given no details; she merely said she must see him urgently on a most important matter. If he assumed it had to do with the diamonds, that was his business.

He came at a quarter to nine, trying to suppress a smile of triumph. Caro assumed he had heard of her disgrace at Lady Brockley's ball; he thought she was going to beg for his help. Who could have told him so soon? And why the deuce should he be smiling about it?

He bowed and came in. "Good morning, ma'am. I had your note. I see you are ready to act sensibly now, after last night's fiasco."

She greeted him with a cool "Good morning,

Dolmain. Good of you to come," and nodded him to a chair. He chose to sit not across from her, but beside her. "Who told you?" she asked, reining in her temper.

"I stopped in at Brockley's around midnight and heard you had been frozen out. Everyone spoke of it. Naturally I squashed the rumor, to the best of my ability. It will be laid to rest for good and all when we are seen out together this evening."

A dangerous spark glowed in her eyes. "You are too kind, but I did not invite you here to gloat, milord."

"If that is the impression I gave, then I am sorry, but I did tell you—"

"Don't you dare say 'I told you so,' in that perfectly odious way," she said angrily.

His lips drew together and his nostrils pinched in disdain. "Then perhaps you will be kind enough to tell me why I have been summoned here when I am really extraordinarily busy at the House."

"I thought I ought to tell you your daughter was at the Pantheon last night and returned home in a carriage with a man, unaccompanied by a chaperon," she said bluntly, purposely avoiding the kinder word, "gentleman."

Dolmain's color heightened from tan to a flushed rose. "Nonsense," he said firmly. "You are mistaken. I might have known you had not the sense to go home, when you were snubbed by society, but only exacerbated the matter by running off to the disreputable Pantheon, to mingle with rakes and rattles and lightskirts."

"And your daughter," she added coldly.

"My daughter was not there, nor should you have been. Julian was always a deal too lax with you."

She was on her feet, eyes shooting sparks. "I am surprised you think me out of place with lightskirts. And how dare you criticize my husband! He was not a toplofty bore like you, to be

54

sure. He knew how to enjoy life. And for your information, I never attended the Pantheon when Julian was alive."

Dolmain did not stand up, but put his hand on her arm and lightly pushed her back onto her chair. "Then it is strange you should go now. It is no fit place for anyone who calls herself a lady."

"I agree it is not the thing, but if it was questionable for a lady of my years and experience to attend, accompanied by a trusted cousin, then you must own it was much worse for a debutante to be there with a man no one has ever heard of."

"Helen attended a musical soirée last night with Miss Blanchard, her French instructress, who makes her home with us. The concert was in aid of the French émigrés. Helen interests herself in their cause, because of her mama."

"So that is who Miss Blanchard is!" Caroline exclaimed. "But why on earth did she send Helen home alone?"

Anger, and perhaps fear, momentarily robbed Dolmain of common sense. He said in a loud voice, "I don't know what you hope to gain by spreading this malicious slander, but if you repeat it outside of this room, I shall—"

"Accuse me of stealing your necklace?" she shot back. "You have already done that."

"I did not accuse you! I have told everyone who quizzed me that I was convinced you are innocent."

"They never would have suspected me in the first place if you had not gone bruiting it about town. And if I planned to spread the truth about your daughter's being at the Pantheon, I would hardly have called you first to inform you. I acted out of the kindness of my heart, for I felt you would naturally want to put a stop to it. She was there, I tell you. I followed them to see the scoundrel did take her home, and not spirit her off to Gretna Green—or worse. This is the thanks I get."

55

"This is impossible," he said, flinging his hands about in consternation. "Helen hasn't a mischievous bone in her body. Anyone will tell you she is a studious girl, well behaved."

"And headstrong. What I say is true. Mr. Newton was with me. You can ask him. There was a Miss Blanchard there, but she did not return to Curzon Street with them. The man—Bernard was his name—took Lady Helen home. Not in your carriage, by the by. She let herself in with a key. The butler must have seen her."

"My butler was ill in bed last night. Miss Blanchard took the house key with her. Helen was aware of it, of course. I did not question what carriage Miss Blanchard planned to use. I assumed it would be my older town carriage, as I had taken my new one myself when I went out."

"There was no crest on the carriage. We tried to follow Bernard when he left your house, but lost him at the corner. Are you interested to hear what else I learned?"

His darkling stare was enough to send chills down her spine, but she tossed her head boldly and stared him down.

"What is it?" he demanded impatiently.

She told him about the money Lady Helen had mentioned, and that she hoped to see someone, some woman or girl, in London. "Have you any idea who it could be?"

He tossed up his hands in confusion. "There was a neighbor who was repining that she could not make her bows, but Helen is hardly in a position to send her that kind of money. And how would Mary explain it to her mama? No, it cannot be that. You must have misunderstood. How did you come to overhear this conversation?"

She was reluctant to tell him, but no other means of having overheard it occurred to her, so she told the simple truth. He stared at her as if she

56

were a Bedlamite. When she finished, he hardly knew whether to thank her or tell her she was mad. But he did believe she was telling the truth. What had she to gain by such a bizarre story?

"If Miss Blanchard has so far abandoned her duties as to do what you say, then naturally I shall dismiss her. It is hard to believe she would behave so irresponsibly. She came to us highly recommended and has given three years of more than satisfactory service."

"I am only telling you what I saw, and heard."

He rose stiffly. On this occasion, Caroline had not offered him coffee. "I thank you for your—intervention," he said, biting back the word *interference*. "In future it will not be necessary for you to follow my daughter. I cannot like to think of you pelting through the streets, hiding behind hedges and eavesdropping on private conversations on my account. I shall undertake to see that Helen behaves properly."

"You are welcome," she said, and mentally added, *It will be a cold day in hell when I put myself out for you or your daughter again, sir.*

Before leaving, he stopped a moment, then said, "Was Helen wearing a mask last night?"

"Yes. I don't believe anyone else recognized her, but it was most assuredly Lady Helen."

His face, which had already shown signs of strain when he arrived, was positively haggard now. He drew a deep sigh and rubbed a hand over his jaw.

"I am truly grateful that you kept an eye on Helen, and told me. I simply do not understand what she can have been doing there. It is entirely out of character."

Caroline felt a weakening urge to console him. "Perhaps there is some simple explanation," she said.

"There must be an explanation, but I doubt it can be simple. I really am extremely sorry I made such

57

a pother about the necklace—that I mentioned your name, I mean. In the turmoil of losing it, I was demmed indiscreet in my questioning of Lady Castlereagh and her servants. It would ease matters for you if you would let me escort you somewhere tonight. I should enjoy it. Let us go out together," he said eagerly.

She was tempted by his persuasions, but to go out with him again could only spell trouble. Because in spite of the way he had treated her, she was still attracted to him. It was impossible to look at his rugged face and strong body without feeling some physical attraction, and his troubled state appealed to her womanly compassion.

"I do not consider myself quite sunk yet, Dolmain. I have arranged to attend the play at Covent Garden with Lady Georgiana this evening. I cannot like to disappoint her."

"I have hired a box for the Season. May I do myself the honor of joining you at intermission?"

This would show society she enjoyed his friendship without the necessity of further entanglement. "I look forward to it." Her tense face eased into a rueful smile. "I must warn you, you will probably be the only caller."

She read an answering softness in his reply. "Was it very bad last night?"

"Wretched. What were people saying after I left?"

"That Countess Caro was always a hurly-burly girl. There was talk of heavy gambling losses at Waite's gaming hell."

"I lost my quarter allowance there five years ago. I have not been back since. What long memories people have. I expect the inference was that I had taken to nabbing my friends' jewels to make up my losses?"

"Something of the sort. If worse comes to worst, I shall have a paste copy of the necklace made and have Helen wear it a few times. That, along with our being seen together on the best of terms, should squelch the rumors."

"Hmm, and make it very easy for the thief to sell the genuine necklace," she cautioned.

Dolmain tilted his head to one side and peered at her. "I had foreseen a different difficulty. Folks would say I had managed to recover it from your grasping fingers, and you had used your wiles to convince me to sponsor you back into society." She could do it, too. The lady was an enchantress, part innocent girl, part vixen. He could not decide which Caro he preferred.

"That is just what they would say! It is odd how the aroma of disrepute hangs on, once it has been acquired."

"If you are trying to make me feel guilty, Caro—" He stopped with a conscious look when he realized he had used her nickname.

Caro looked surprised, but did not reprimand him. "Perhaps it is your conscience that is doing that," she said. The air grew still as they stared at each other. Neither spoke, but he read the accusation in her gaze, and felt, suddenly, not only guilty, but small. Then she put her hand on his arm and accompanied him from the room.

"I think you should leave before we come to cuffs again, Dolmain. We have pulled one crow already, and it is only nine o'clock. You must keep some of your bile to spurt at the illustrious members of the Horse Guards."

"Is it nine o'clock already? How time flies when we are enjoying ourselves," he said, with a deprecating grin.

"Yes indeed. If you had come with a summons for my arrest, I daresay we would be rolling in laughter by now. When they clamp me in irons, I expect you will have a ball to celebrate."

"A ball would be no pleasure without you, Caro," he said. He had meant to use a light tone, and was surprised at how sincere he sounded. Caro looked at him with a question in her eyes.

Before she could think of an answer, they had reached the front door. Crumm's scarred face peered around the corner. Caroline shook her head to indicate he was not required.

"It's a beautiful day," Dolmain said, rather wistfully. "I wish we could drive into the country again. I have the whole day booked. If I hope to make it to the theater for the first intermission tonight, I had best get to work."

"I did not realize your only reason for going was to redeem my reputation. You must not let that interfere with your work, Dolmain. England's safety takes precedence over my reputation." Yet she was touched at his efforts on her behalf.

"Redeeming your reputation is not the only reason. After looking at York and Hotchkiss and the rest of the ugly members of the Horse Guards, my poor eyes deserve a reward."

"I hear Esmée, the new actress, is quite lovely."

"Very likely, but I had not actually planned to remain for the play."

She made a playful curtsey. "A pretty compliment, sir."

She opened the door. Dolmain pinched her chin, said, "Don't give up. We'll solve this riddle yet." Then he was gone.

Nothing had really changed much, yet Caroline's heart felt lighter. A problem was not so heavy a burden when it was shared. She wished with all her heart that the necklace had not intruded itself into their lives. It had seemed, for a day or two, that she had found someone to replace Julian. . . .

Chapter Seven

At ten o'clock Lady Georgiana came to breakfast and was told the gist of Dolmain's visit.

She just shook her head. "I used to think you were one of those ladies who attracted trouble and attention, as honey attracts flies, but I was mistaken. You go to meet it halfway, Caro. It was not necessary for you to follow Lady Helen home, though it was proper of you to notify Lord Dolmain today."

"Something might have happened to her," Caro pointed out.

"So it might, and it was kind of you to watch her, but to go creeping behind bushes, and then to tell Lord Dolmain you had done so! He will think you no better than a hoyden. You must not forget discretion in your wholesale acts of kindness."

"Dolmain was grateful. He will make a special trip to Covent Garden tonight to visit our box, to show his support."

"Let him come, and let him accompany you to some formal do to show the world he trusts you. He owes you that much. After that, leave Dolmain to handle his own troubles. It seems to me there is something havey-cavey afoot. You are best out of it."

"You have done your duty, shrew," Caro said, softening her words with a smile.

"Who am I to give advice? I have made a confounded mess of my own life."

"How can you say so? You have never been in a pickle."

"That is precisely what I mean. I have lived vicariously. It is comfortable, but there is no denying it can become boring at times. Now that I am older, I wish I had a few scrapes and pickles to look back on."

"You are welcome to share mine," Caro said ruefully.

"I am afraid I must pass. It is time for my daily constitutional, accompanied by my beau," Georgie said. This was a joking reference to the footman who would accompany her. Lady Georgiana was one of the sights of Rotten Row, where she rode for an hour every day, rain or shine, mounted on a bay mare.

Georgie had no sooner left than Newton was shown into the saloon. "What are you up to today, Newt?" Caroline asked.

"Thought I might stop off at Manton's and culp a wafer—or miss it, more like. Then a round at Jackson's Parlor to refresh my science."

"Setting up as a Corinthian?" Caroline asked. Neither shooting nor boxing had ever featured in his life before, except as spectator sports. "Who is she? It must be a lady who has driven you to this extremity."

No effort was too great when Newt was on the scent of a new love. He had once studied the piano for six months to woo a musically inclined lady. Another time he had turned Methodist, and given up dancing and music entirely. The object of his affection on that occasion had abandoned her strict religion and run off with a caper merchant.

"Ain't a lady. It's a gentleman," he said.

"Ah, and whom are you emulating this time? Lord Byron, is it? I hear he takes lessons of Gentleman Jackson."

"I don't think it's Byron. He don't drag his foot, the fellow I am talking about. Sets a lively pace."

"Don't you know his name?"

"No, nor his face. I just know he is always there, a few paces behind me, dogging my footsteps like a dashed shadow. If he turns rusty, I must be ready to defend myself."

Eliciting hard facts from Newt was never easy. "Tell me all about him," she urged.

"I first spotted him last night. Did you happen to notice the carriage following us?"

"No, I didn't. When did it start?"

"I figure he must have followed us from the Pantheon. I first caught a sight of him lurking at the corner when I came out of your place after bringing you home. Hadn't noticed him before that, but he must have followed me there. He ran to his rig and followed me to the Albany. Then when I went out this morning, there he was, tailing me again. Drives a plain black carriage. I noticed him as I rounded the bend to your street. Daresay he was behind me all the while, only the traffic was so thick, I could not spot him. Followed me here."

"Who can he be?" Caroline dashed to the window.

"Wasting your time," Newt informed her. "He waits around the corner. Take a peek when I leave. You'll see he's not a block behind me. Pair of bays, one with white stockings on her forelegs."

"That is very odd. What do you think he wants with you?"

"No idea. I ain't in dun territory. Haven't insulted anyone that I know of. I figure it must be to do with Lady Helen. Mean to say, it all started at the Pantheon."

"Let us go out, *tout de suite*, and see if he follows us."

"That is just what I have been saying to you. The *tout*er the better. Get your wrapper and let us go."

Of course, he had not said anything of the sort,

but no doubt he had been trying to say it. Caroline got her bonnet and pelisse and they went out to Newton's waiting carriage. Before they turned the first corner, the plain black carriage, pulled by a pair of bays, rounded the bend and followed them. For an hour they led it a merry chase, first north to Oxford Street, where the traffic was not too heavy, then to High Holborn, south along Drury Lane to the Strand and on to the Mall. At St. James's Park they alit and walked, to allow them a look at the man in the carriage.

He was as anonymous as his vehicle: a man of middle size and middle years, neither old nor young, wearing a blue jacket and tan trousers. He was a gentleman, or at least dressed like one. Caroline was all for accosting him and demanding why he was following them.

Newton said, "He'll not tell us anything. Best to play dumb, let on we don't know he is there. Sooner or later I'll find the opportunity to get away from him. I plan to follow him and see where he goes. Might be a clue."

"I suppose you are right. How can we lose him?"

"I shall go back to Manton's, ask Joe to let me slip out the back door, and have a hired hansom waiting. I'll let you know what I find out this evening. Are we still on for Covent Garden?"

"Yes, it is all arranged. Georgie wants to use my carriage to pick up her friends, so I shall go in yours, if that's all right?"

"Right. I'll take you home now."

She watched from her saloon window when Newton left but did not see the carriage follow him.

Caro related her morning exploits to her sister-in-law over lunch.

"But the man did not follow Newt when he left?" she asked.

"No, I watched for quite ten minutes. He must have circled around some other way."

"Your wits are gone begging, Caro," Georgie said, with a sharp look. "It is not Newton he is following. It is you. Newton said he first noticed the carriage when he brought you home last night. And this morning when he called on you, it was at your corner again. He did not follow Newt here; he was here watching your house. I wager he is still lurking around the corner even as we speak."

"Good God! Why would anyone be watching me?"

"Newton was right about one thing. It has to do with that visit to the Pantheon last night. And perhaps with the vanished necklace as well."

Caroline sat, momentarily stunned into silence. Her frown slowly faded, to be replaced by a diabolical smile. "I shall be going out to New Bond Street this afternoon, Georgie. Will you come with me? You are always complaining of a lack of excitement. My shadow might provide us some amusement."

"Oh, I couldn't!" Georgiana exclaimed, but there was an unaccustomed note of excitement in her voice.

"Why not? He cannot harm us in the middle of London. I shall try Newton's ruse of escaping the man, and following him to see where he goes."

"You still carry that pistol in the side pocket of your rig?"

"Always, and I know how to use it, too."

Two spots of red burned high on Georgiana's sallow cheeks. "I'll do it!" she said, and laughed a tinny laugh.

Immediately after lunch the ladies dressed and had the carriage brought around. Watching from the rear window, they saw the dark carriage turn the corner and follow them when they left.

"This all began at the Pantheon last night," Caroline said, smiling wickedly. "We shall lose him at the Pantheon Bazaar. Miss Millar will let us slip out her back door. I buy a deal of ribbon and lace from her. We shall have a hansom cab waiting for us there. The footman can arrange it while John Groom minds the carriage. My shadow will stick with the carriage, I think."

They followed this plan. Miss Millar, who operated a drapery shop at the Pantheon Bazaar, was entirely agreeable to helping out a good customer. She would have assumed Lady Winbourne was arranging a romantic tryst, were it not for the old malkin with her. Caroline and Georgiana spent ten minutes rooting through trays of lace. At the end of that time, Miss Millar beckoned them to the rear of the store.

"The hired hack is here, your ladyship."

"Thank you, Miss Millar," Caro said, dropping a coin into her hand. "If a nondescript gentleman comes in here asking for me, don't tell him I have left. You are quite busy, so you can pretend you did not notice me."

"Oh lawks, your ladyship. Just like a play on the stage. I'll not whiddle the scrap."

"Thank you."

They slipped out the back door to the hired carriage and asked the groom to drive around and wait a half block away. They pointed out the carriage he was to follow, at a discreet distance. It was a long wait. Their pursuer could not believe Lady Caroline had tipped him the double. He went from shop to shop, peering in at the windows. After half an hour, he knew she had given him the slip and returned to his own rig.

"There, he is leaving now!" Caroline said, and pulled the drawstring to alert the driver.

To her considerable consternation, the carriage they were following drove to Berkeley Square, where it circled the block, obviously awaiting her return. She managed to foil him to the extent of scampering into her own house unseen while he was around the corner, but she had still not learned where he came from.

"Who can he be? Why is he following me?" she asked.

"I cannot imagine," Georgiana said.

"It must have to do with Lady Helen and the necklace. The man will surely not watch the house all night. He must sleep sometime, like everyone else. I shall have a footman follow him when he leaves. We must get to the bottom of this. It is driving me mad."

Lady Georgiana said, "I must own, I rather enjoyed it, Caro. What a lot of fun I have been missing all these years by my caution."

"I would hardly call it fun. The fun will come when I learn who the scoundrel is and why he is following me. I do look forward to that. And now let us prepare for the evening."

Lady Georgiana's guests for the theater were all either widows, or spinsters, like herself. A night at the theater was a rare festive occasion for them. Georgiana left in Caroline's carriage shortly after dinner to pick them up.

Newt came in a few moments later, shaking his head. "Something deuced odd going on," he said. "I thought the fellow had let up following me. Not a sign of him all afternoon, but just now I spotted him again, loitering about at the corner of Berkeley Square like a dashed hedge bird."

"It is not you he is following; it is me," she said, and told him of her afternoon's work.

Newton did not wipe his brow, but his "That is a relief!" gave that impression. "Thought I had figured it out. Taylor."

"You said you are not in dun territory."

"Not a coat-maker. Jack Taylor. Had a bit of a run-in with him over a game of cards. Took him for a monkey, fair and square. He wanted a chance to recoup. It was four o'clock in the morning. I could hardly prop my peepers open. I offered to meet him another time. Said he had to rusticate, pockets to let. What have you been up to, that someone is following you?"

"I hope to shed some light on that tonight." She outlined her plan of having the fellow followed by a footman after she returned from the theater.

"Footman!" he exclaimed in high dudgeon. "Dash it, I shall follow him myself. Easy as chopping off a log. I'll catch the oiler. I can run like a stag if I have to. We'll get to the bottom of this yet."

She put on her mantle and they left for the theater.

Chapter Eight

The subtitle of Mr. Sheridan's comedy *The Critic*, which Caroline and Georgiana were attending that evening, was *A Tragedy Rehearsed*. Caroline felt the second title was more appropriate to her situation. Until the curtain opened, it seemed the major drama was occurring in her box on the upper tier. Why else did so many ladies train their opera glasses on her, and so many gentlemen raise their quizzing glasses? Those quizzing glasses could not have aided vision much, but did lend a fine condemnatory air.

When Newt saw her distress, he said, "Won't the gawpers stare on the other side of their faces when Dolmain joins us."

This finally brought a trembling smile to Caroline's lips.

She paid little heed to the carrying on of Dangle and Sneer, the spiteful critics. Her mind was occupied with private problems. She would ask Dolmain to accompany her out to the corridor for wine. They would laugh and joke and show the world they were the best of friends. That should silence *her* critics.

When Georgiana attended the theater, it was her custom to have wine brought to the box for the first intermission, rather than leave her seat. When the curtain fell, Caroline sat, waiting for Dolmain's arrival. Her box was not totally ignored. A few of Georgie's cronies dropped in, and some of Caroline's friends came to invite her to walk with them. She explained that she was waiting for a friend. But as the minutes dragged on and the audience began straggling back to their seats, she realized that Dolmain was not coming. He had taken her at her word that she did not need his protection—or he had changed his mind. Either way, she felt betrayed. If he had any concern for her, he would have come. He knew how she had suffered last night at Brockley's ball.

The second act was agony. Had it not been for Georgie, she would have left early. Newton tried manfully to amuse her by poking her elbow at each witticism and exclaiming, "That was a good one, eh?" She could hardly muster an acknowledgment. What would happen to her if society ostracized her? She could never see Dolmain; they would no longer frequent the same do's. He would not have her even as a friend if she became an outcast. He had his daughter's reputation to consider. As he had said, a lost reputation was difficult to recover. Some shadow of guilt would always hover over her head. She would be "not quite the thing," not invited to the best homes. Almack's would be closed to her as a matter of course. The toplofty Mrs. Drummond Burrell would see to that. This grande dame had once chided her and Julian for laughing too loudly at the club, and Julian had snubbed her.

"Is this not a party? Or has someone died, ma'am?" he had asked, in his mischievous way. "I thought Lord Buten looked particularly moribund. You ought to have had the knocker done up in crepe."

Oh yes, Mrs. Burrell would be very happy to turn her off.

When the second intermission came, Georgie said, "We shall take a short stroll to stretch our legs. Do come with us, Caro. It will do you good."

"I could not bear it, Georgie," Caroline replied in

a low voice. "Perhaps my friends will come again. Newt has offered to remain with me."

"We shan't be long," Georgie said, and went out with her group.

Newton looked at Caroline from under his eyebrows and said, "You are looking lonely as a crowd, Caro. I could go out and round up a group if you like."

Even Newt's mangling of the mother tongue no longer amused her. "I shan't go running after society," she said. "If they don't want me, then I don't want them."

"Want to change tails and run home, then?"

"No, I shall stay until the end."

He pointed across the hall. "There, Miss Simcoe is waving at you."

Caroline waved back, grateful for any support.

"Let me get some wine at least," was his next suggestion. "This smiling and letting on you are having a good time is tiresome work."

She dreaded being left alone, yet it seemed hard to deny Newt a glass of wine after his help. "Yes, go ahead," she said.

"Buck up, my girl. You've got to take the bitter with the sour."

He was just leaving when the door to her box opened and Lord Dolmain stepped in. He was there, distinguished, above reproach, smiling, and making a gallant bow in full view of all her scorners. Such a wave of gratitude welled up inside her that she feared she would cry. He did care for her a little. Oh, and she did love him, try as she might to fight the knowledge.

"Good evening, Dolmain," she said, blinking back a tear.

"A thousand pardons," he said. "Work ran late at the House. I could not make it for the first intermission."

"That is quite all right," she replied in a voice trembling with relief.

The sight of her pinched, pale face filled him with remorse. Almost worse was to see her behave so submissively. The old Caro would have given him a good Bear Garden jaw for being late. What had he done to her? The lovely, carefree Caro looked as if she carried the weight of the world on her dainty shoulders. He wanted to carry her off to safety, to pamper and protect her. She couldn't be guilty! Oh Lord, this could not be *love* he felt. But he knew when he saw her moist eyes that he would do anything to see her smile again in her old, carefree way.

"I'll run along and get the wine, then," Newton said, and left.

Dolmain said, "May I?" and dropped into the seat beside her.

As Caroline glanced out at the theater, she saw the shocked expressions on her erstwhile critics. Weren't they smiling now, and trying to catch her attention! They were like lemmings, led hither or thither without thinking for themselves.

Dolmain cast an eye on the nearly empty box and said, "This is an unaccustomed sight! Lady Winbourne without her court. Have the demmed jackanapes all deserted you? Good riddance," he said contemptuously. "I have you all to myself."

"It was kind of you to come," she said in a chastened voice.

"It was the least I could do, as I am responsible for your being ostracized," he replied grimly. "I should like to stay here alone with you, but it would be best if we circulate."

"Yes, that might be best," she agreed reluctantly.

They went into the corridor. The first reaction was a strained silence, as heads turned and people stared, almost in disbelief.

"Now I know how you must have felt at Brockley's ball," Dolmain said.

"And I know how the wild animals at Exeter Exchange must feel," she replied. It was really too ludicrous. She laughed in mingled relief and amusement at the world's folly.

"That is more like it," he said, squeezing her arm.

As the crowd assimilated the sight of Dolmain and Lady Winbourne, chatting and laughing together, they came surging forward, some swiftly, some at a lagging gait, some swept along by the tide. It seemed the half of the audience of Covent Garden was suddenly gathered around Caroline and Dolmain. Not liking to say what had been in their minds, they spoke of the play instead. A marvelous comedy. Sheridan was so witty, there was no matching him.

Ladies who had known Caroline for a decade found themselves saying foolishly, "I was not sure that was you with Lady Georgiana."

"Yes, in the same box we have had these many years," Caroline replied demurely. She could not refrain from one little gibe.

She felt Dolmain's fingers tighten on her elbow in warning. This was not the time for revenge, but for repairing fences.

It was Lady Jersey, the greatest chatterbox in London, and the rudest, who said, "Can we assume that you have recovered Lady Helen's diamonds, Dolmain, as you and Caro are so cozy?"

Dolmain gave her a lazy smile. "I have a fellow looking into it," he replied nonchalantly, and immediately rushed on to compliment her on her toilette.

When Lady Jersey, called Silence as a compliment to her running tongue, opened her lips to ask more pointed questions about the necklace, Dolmain said, "Excuse me, we have friends waiting in our box. Shall we go, Caro?"

Caroline felt a rush of pleasure to hear him refer to her in this intimate way in front of Silence, as if they had been bosom bows forever. Only her best friends called her Caro.

He ushered her back toward the box, saying, "Did you want to walk more? We can scoot around the corner to escape Jersey if you like. Leave it to her to blurt out what everyone was thinking, but was too polite to say. Silence never stops talking long enough to think."

"Let us return to the box," she said. "I did want an opportunity to talk to you in private."

"Later, when we are away from this audience. Now we must speak of nothings. Are you enjoying the play?"

"I could hardly tell you what I have been watching, my mind is in such a turmoil."

"Then I have a suggestion to make. Leave with me now. We have been seen; if you are missing from your box for the last act, folks will assume we have gone off together. That will confirm the notion that we are bosom bows. It will give us an opportunity for that talk.

She was only too happy to leave. "Very well, but I must tell Newt."

They went to take their leave of Newton, and to ask him to tell Georgiana that Caroline had gone home with Dolmain.

"You don't mind?" Caroline asked him.

"Just as you like. All the more wine for me," was his easy reply.

The audience were returning to their boxes as Caroline and Dolmain left the theater. Several people saw them and passed the word along. It was pretty well known they had left together even before scanning Caro's box after the second intermission.

Chapter Nine

As Dolmain accompanied her to his carriage, he said, "You must wonder why I have two footmen mounted behind the carriage. I am as safely guarded as a vestal virgin. The Duke of York, at the Horse Guards, you know, has insisted we all be escorted since we are such important fellows. The success of the war in the Peninsula rests on our shoulders."

She gave him a pert smile. "I seem to have heard a certain Lord Wellington is in charge of things there."

"Yes, when he can get our set off his shoulders. It was his influence that got a few of us Whigs into the Horse Guards, to curb the more sublime idiocies of York and his boys. York feels the conduct of war is too important to leave to generals and officers. It requires the fine hand and superior brainpower of people like us who have never seen a war, or ever been in Spain."

As he rattled on in this light vein, he ushered her into the carriage, where he sat beside her. As soon as they were comfortably ensconced in its velvet bosom, he became serious.

"What was it you wished to discuss, Caro?"

"Someone has been following me," she said, and told him about Newt's discovery, and her testing of it.

He frowned. "Let us drive a little out of town and see if he is still on your trail when we get away

75

from traffic." He opened the window and called the new order to his groom.

"Meanwhile, tell me what Lady Helen and Miss Blanchard had to say about last night when you spoke to them," she said.

"Miss Blanchard admits she allowed Helen to prevail on her to skip the concert and go to the Pantheon. It was wrong of her, but I do not hold Miss Blanchard entirely to blame. Helen can be persuasive. She would have sneaked away on her own sooner or later. Miss Blanchard thought it best for her to take Helen, so that she would at least be guarded. Helen had heard her friends speak of the Pantheon as one of the sights of London, and in her innocence had no notion what it is like. It was an error in judgment. It won't be repeated."

"What is Miss Blanchard's excuse for sending Helen home alone with that man? And who is he?"

"A perfectly safe fellow. He is Miss Blanchard's cousin, Pierre Bernard. She followed behind them in my rig. She did not want anyone to see Helen climbing into my rig, in case the carriage was recognized. That was thoughtful of her."

"It would have been more thoughtful had she accompanied Helen in her cousin's rig, and he taken your carriage."

"So it would, but she did not think of that. Helen convinced me to forgive her this one lapse and keep her on. Every dog has his bite, as the saying goes. I made it perfectly clear she is not to do that sort of thing again."

He then changed the subject. "Let us see if this mysterious rig is following you now." He peered out the window. Seeing nothing, he had the carriage stopped and asked his groom to keep an eye out.

They drove again out the Chelsea Road. The deserted countryside was eerie by moonlight. Tall trees took on a menacing aspect as their branches swayed and bent in the breeze. A ghostly moon floated high above in the infinite black sky, surrounded by a wilderness of stars.

Caroline felt a shiver lift the hair on her arms. "There might be highwaymen. Let us go home," she said.

"I thought we might stop for a late supper. There is an inn a mile down the road that serves good food—the Hound and Hind. We worked through the dinner hour at the Horse Guards. We had sandwiches sent in, but I am in the mood for a beefsteak."

She felt a rush of concern for Dolmain, working so hard and so selflessly. Buoyed by his support at Covent Garden, she was in a mood for some amusement. It was the impulsive, spur-of-the-moment sort of thing she and Julian used to do.

"I shall join you, but not in a beefsteak. I shall have chicken, or perhaps a raised pigeon pie. To tell the truth, I have not eaten much today myself, with all these worries—"

Dolmain was overcome in a wave of remorse. "Caro, my dear!" On an impulse, he drew her into his arms and cuddled her against his chest, stroking her head to comfort her. Her hair was like finest silk. A light scent of flowers wafted up to enchant him. She felt dainty, all soft curves, femininely alluring, nestled in his arms. He was overcome with remorse for the ordeal he had put her through. And he called himself a gentleman!

"I feel a perfect monster, Caro," he said. "This is all my fault. The last thing I wanted to do was hurt you."

He continued stroking her. As he soothed away her worries, she felt a warmth growing inside her. When he put his fingers beneath her chin and tilted her head up, she gazed at his face, bathed in shadowy moonlight. An honest, masculine face. A shiver of anticipation trembled up her spine as his head inclined slowly to hers, and she read the intention in his eyes. He was going to kiss her, but like a gentleman, he was waiting to see if she objected. She lifted her warm lips to his. The reaction was like a spark to tinder. After the first light touch, his arms crushed her against his hard chest. As his lips firmed, bruising hers in a ruthless kiss, she felt as if her lungs had collapsed, sending her heart up to pound in her throat. It had been so long since she had felt this fever in the blood. Three years of pent-up passion flooded through her like a tidal wave as she returned every ardent pressure.

When she finally drew away, she felt embarrassed at having let herself go. "Georgie is always telling me I am too impulsive," she said breathlessly. "Too quick to anger, and too quick to—" She swallowed the word *love*, which had nearly escaped.

"I have not been accused of that—until now," he said, and lifting her hand, he placed a kiss on her fingers. "For myself, I prefer a lady with spirit. Ah, we have reached the Hound and Hind."

Caro didn't know whether she was glad or sorry.

They were led to a private parlor, with a table laid in the center of the room, a cozy fire blazing in the grate, and a sofa in front of it. They had a glass of wine by the fire while awaiting their dinner.

Dolmain seemed to relish his beefsteak. Caroline certainly enjoyed her chicken. It was simple country cooking, but prepared with care. A French ragout could not have been more welcome. When the servants cleared away the table, Dolmain said, "Now a bottle of champagne to cap a lovely evening."

"I should be getting home," Caro said reluctantly. This latter part of the evening had been so enjoyable, she was sorry to see it end.

"*Carpe diem*, Caro," he said, gazing at her with a question in his eyes. "Seize the day. If this . . . experience . . . has taught me anything, it is that we should enjoy ourselves while we can. There is no saying what misfortune lurks around the corner, waiting to attack."

She thought of his work, so dangerous that the Duke of York had assigned him two bodyguards. He could be dead tomorrow. But she mistrusted that glint in his eyes. She was a widow, and widows were considered fair game by some gentlemen. Was it possible Dolmain put her in that category? If so, she must show him he was mistaken.

"I really must be going home," she said firmly.

"You're right. It is rather late," he said, trying to conceal his disappointment. That warm embrace in the carriage had misled him. Yet he was not really sorry that Caro was unavailable for an affair. What she required was a husband.

They drove home, still friends, with her head resting on his shoulder. His arms enfolding her felt natural and right, and wonderfully protective. She had often felt vulnerable since Julian's passing. Gentlemen who behaved themselves when he was alive were inclined to take liberties after his death. She had learned to depress them, but life was more comfortable with a male protector. She hardly knew what she would have done if Dolmain had not come to the theater.

As they approached London, Dolmain looked out the window. "I don't see anyone following," he said.

She had forgotten all about the man following her.

"We shall go somewhere together tomorrow evening," he said. It wasn't a question, nor quite a command.

She gazed at him, interested. "Yes," she said.

When they reached Berkeley Square, he accompanied her to the door for a good-night kiss.

Crumm met her at the door. "Mr. Newton is waiting for you. We was about to call out Bow Street," he added severely.

"I went for a drive with Lord Dolmain," she said.

"Is that what he called it? It looked like cuddling to me. I had half a mind to darken his daylights."

"Your duties stop at the door, Crumm," she replied.

Newton came out of the saloon to meet her. His inflated chest gave him the air of a pouter pigeon. It was a sign that he had some important discovery to reveal.

"Well, I have solved one mystery at least," he announced.

"What is that?" she asked, putting off her mantle.

"The fellow who was following you."

"He did not follow me tonight."

"No, he followed me," he said, refreshing his glass of wine and pouring one for Caroline. "Thought you was in my rig, likely, since I drove you to the theater."

"Did you discover who he is?"

"No, but I know who hired him. I drove round here to your place and stopped. Ducked into the house before he made it around the corner so he would think I had seen you into the house. Had my rig circle the block, slipped out the back door and met it at the corner. Followed the rig that had been following me. It went to Curzon Street. It is Dolmain that he is reporting to."

"Don't be ridiculous," she scoffed.

Newt directed an owlish look at her disheveled hair. "I see he has been sweet-talking you. You don't want to believe all he says, Caro. No, not a half of it. He is having you followed. In other words, he thinks you stole his necklace."

Caroline's heart shrank within her. It seemed impossible, but common sense told her it must be so. All his solicitude about trying to discover who was following her—it was just a pretext to get her to the Hound and Hind for the ultimate revenge. She had not been mistaken about his meaning when he suggested champagne to celebrate. Celebrate what? They had not found the necklace. He was trying to prove her a thief. Her first regret soon congealed to anger. She had to fuel her anger to keep her heart from breaking.

"He has been at you, hasn't he?" Newt asked angrily.

"We went for a drive out the Chelsea Road. Dolmain said it would be easier to see if I was being followed away from the traffic. We stopped for supper. We were both hungry."

Newt sniffed. "He knew you wasn't being followed. Next you will be telling me he took you to the Hound and Hind!"

"Why do you say that?" she asked.

"Good Lord, Caro, it is as well known as an old ballad that all the gents take their high-class mistresses there. Nice and private, out of town, so no one will see them." He looked at her ashen face. "He didn't take you there?" he asked in a hollow voice.

"Yes, but we didn't—"

"The scoundrel! I have a good mind to call him out. Only I will need a second."

"Not a duel! Good God, that would finish me forever. I have become shady enough without that."

"True. The deuce of it is, without his support, you are a social outcast. Mean to say, we have no chance of finding out what happened to the necklace if no one will speak to you."

And that meant she must keep her tongue between her teeth. She must smile and smirk at the hateful Lord Dolmain until she discovered who had taken the diamonds. Then she would tell him exactly what she thought of him.

After a little discussion, it was decided that Caro would pretend she was unaware of Dolmain's ploy. She would go out with him tomorrow evening as planned, but she would not let him pierce her defenses again.

Crumm peered in at the door. "Your carriage is here," he said to Newton.

"I had my groom follow the fellow who was following me," Newt explained. "I legged it home from Curzon Street. Dolmain was not there, so Ankel had to wait. He will tell us where the scoundrel lives."

"Ask him in. I would like to hear this," Caro said.

Newt's groom was a small, wiry, dark-visaged man with a lock of black hair curling on his forehead.

"Well, what did you learn?" Newt demanded.

Ankel bobbed his head at Lady Winbourne. "The lad as was following us waited at Curzon Street until Lord Dolmain landed home. Five minutes after his lordship went in, out comes t'other lad, wearing a grin and patting his pocket. He was well paid, I'm thinking. Better paid than some," he added with an accusing look at his master.

"Never mind that," Newt said. "Where did the bleater go?"

"To an apartment on Poland Street," Ankel announced. "And I, being awake on all suits, can tell you which set of rooms he went to. After he went in, the lights went on in the third floor. Checked the nameplates. Fellow calls himself Mr. Smith. An alias, very likely, but at least we know where to lay our hands on him. Shall we run along and pummel him a little?"

"That won't be necessary," Caro said in a dull voice.

"You can run along, Ankel," Newt said.

"Was you planning to leg it home?" Ankel asked.

"Wait for me in the rig, gudgeon."

"Never a word o' thanks," Ankel grumbled as he left.

Caroline squeezed Newt's fingers. "What would I do without you?" she said.

Newt preened himself and said modestly, "My pleasure, I'm sure. I always knew you would come a cropper sooner or later. A complete greenhead, even if you have been on the town forever."

On this equivocal speech, he took his leave. Georgiana had still not returned. Her outings, while rare, included a supper that could go on until two or three in the morning. Caro was exhausted and went to bed.

Julian's portrait smiled commiseratingly down at her. "Buck up, my girl," he seemed to say, as he had said countless times in the past when she had incurred society's wrath by straying from the narrow precincts of propriety. "This, too, will pass." But this suspicion of theft could ruin her socially, and Julian's cavalier advice was of little use. A certain recklessness was acceptable in a noble young couple, with the title and estates at their backs. A young dowager, if she ever wished to make another respectable alliance, must be like Caesar's wife, above reproach.

Once her reputation was lost, she would be prey to all manner of unwanted advances. She felt a frisson along her scalp. Did Dolmain already consider her a fallen woman? Was that why he had felt free to take her to that iniquitous den? And here she had thought he was beginning to love her.

Chapter Ten

Caroline received a note from Dolmain the next morning that was part business correspondence, part billet-doux.

Dear Caro: Re this evening, does Lady Sefton's do suit you? Addie Derwent's assembly in aid of the fire victims might be more amusing (she has set up faro tables), but I feel the wiser option is to stick to the haute ton for the present. Also, I plan to take Helen with us, and cannot like to expose her to the faro table at her tender years. Might your cousin, Mr. Newton, like to complete our party? As I am depriving him of his usual partner, the least I can do is supply an alternative. I leave the decision up to you. Any outing with you is bound to be delightful. If you feel strongly about attending Addie's do, we could drop in there after the ball, sans Helen and Newton. I am particularly looking forward to "after the ball." Shall we drive out the Chelsea Road again? Your faithful servant, D.

Caroline read the note with a rising anger. Why did he keep harping on Addie Derwent's faro table, as if she were a confirmed gambler? But it was the mention of "after the ball" that caused her jaw to clench. If he anticipated a repeat of last night's performance, he would be disappointed. She did want to be seen at Lady Sefton's ball on Dolmain's arm, however, so she must remain civil. She was curious to see that Helen would be with them. Newt would be happy to accompany her, and between them, they might discover something from her.

As soon as Newton received her note inviting him to join the party, he called for his carriage and drove to Berkeley Square in a frenzy, steaming at every pore. To her amazement, he entered wearing a bearish scowl.

"If this is a joke, Caro, it ain't funny," he said. "Mean to say, you know I have feelings for Lady Helen, even if her papa is a mawworm."

"Do sit down. Would you care for a drink?"

"Passionately." He ignored the coffeepot and poured himself a glass of wine, which he gulped down like a man who had been stranded in the desert for a week.

"Are you not pleased with the invitation?" Caro asked.

"Thrilled to minced meat. To tell the truth, I am as nervous as a chicken with a fox peering in at the door."

"Nervous of a schoolgirl?"

"True, I have been on the town awhile. Know which side of the street is up." Still his nerves refused to be tamed by mere facts. "Fact is, I am a martyr to self-doubts when it comes to petticoat dealings," he explained. "If she was a filly, I would not have a care in the world. I understand horses, but women! I am head over heels in love with the chit. She is head over heels over shoulders above me. I may not be the sharpest knife in the drawer, but I know that much. All the bucks are dangling after her. I tell myself I am good as any of them— well, as eligible in point of fortune—but it does no good. Goes in one ear and out the other, like a dose of salts," he said, with a very poor notion of anatomy.

When she assured him that Helen had very little

experience of gentlemen and could not be so very demanding, he found a new concern. "What cravat shall I wear? Do you think the Oriental, or is it too big? My face looks like a moon on a platter in those big cravats. I ain't sure my man can do it either. Should I send her a corsage? I don't want to be encroaching."

She calmed him down, talked him out of the Oriental cravat and the Brutus do, which would not at all suit his full face, suggested a modest corsage of baby roses for a young lady just making her debut, and generally assuaged his fears.

"What will I say to her?" was his next concern. "I hope she likes horses. I could talk an hour about my stable."

"Oh, I would not do that, Newt. Ten minutes is quite enough. What you must talk about is that trip to the Pantheon, and the missing diamonds and Miss Blanchard. I am sure Lady Helen knows more than she has told her papa."

"That ought to keep the chat rattling along. I hope she ain't blue. If she starts talking books, I am done for."

With a heavy day ahead of him preparing for the ball, he soon left. By four he had arranged all the details with his valet and was free to drive to Hyde Park. He called on Caro, but she was entertaining her neighbor, Lady Jersey, so he left before that dame tried to induce him to attend Almack's.

His trip to the park was a success. He saw Lady Helen. She was accompanied by Lady Milchamp, but when Helen met up with a group of youngsters to stroll about the park, the chaperon remained in the carriage. Newt pulled in behind her and followed Helen's group, hoping to overhear the conversation, to learn what interested her. His blue eyes narrowed when she fell a little behind the group. He watched as a handsome young scoundrel popped out from behind a tree and spoke to her.

Newton was all set to pounce forward and rescue her from the mushroom when he recognized the fellow. It was that Bernard she had been dancing with at the Pantheon. He and Helen were chatting away, six to the dozen—in French. It might as well have been Dutch as far as Newt was concerned.

He observed every detail of Bernard's toilette. There was no hope of his own body growing six inches or of his brindle hair turning to black in four hours. What he might do was induce a bit of a curl into it. Bernard's glossy black hair fell forward in a wave when he removed his curled beaver.

Helen remained with Bernard for a good ten minutes, until her group returned. When Bernard left, she went back to her carriage with the others. A sly puss, meeting her fellow behind Lady Milchamp's back. Just his luck that Helen already had someone else in her eye. Yet as he considered that meeting, it was not melting looks and soft smiles between them, but quick questions and answers. In fact, Helen had seemed a bit angry with him, but the smooth talker soon pacified her. Something to do with the girl Helen was trying to bring to London, perhaps.

He went home, thinking about Caro's hint that his face was full. A bigger head of hair might lessen the moonlike nature of his face. To this end, he had his valet do his hair up in papers to give it a curl. When the papers were removed, he looked like a Hottentot. Tight brindle corkscrews bounced all over his head, yet his pink cheeks looked as full as ever. His valet removed the curl as much as he could by an application of water, but they bounced back as soon as the hair dried.

It was all Caroline could do not to laugh out loud when she saw how Newt had redecorated himself. His shirt points reached to his ears, to be met by the riot of curls. "I see you have changed your coiffure, Newt," she said in a choked voice.

"What do you think? Take it up and down and all around, what do you think of it? Is it even worse than before?"

The hair could not be changed, and rather than add to his nervousness by disapproving of it, she said, "It looks fine."

"I want to look my best. I hope to offer for her tonight."

"Oh no, Newt! It is too soon. You hardly know her."

"You can't leap a chasm in two jumps. It is now or never. She will soon have met other men; then what chance have I?"

"You have a poor opinion of yourself! But only think, you would have to ask Dolmain's permission first."

"*Partis* ain't exactly thick on the ground. I own an abbey. Come from good stock. I'll do it tonight, if I get the chance."

Caro intended to see he was not left alone with Dolmain. To rush his fence in this manner would ruin any slim chance he might have of winning Helen.

"How do I look?" she asked, to distract his thoughts.

She had changed her coiffure to a more sedate do to lend her an air of dignity. Her raven curls were held back by a silver ribbon and braided à la Didon, emphasizing her high cheekbones and classical nose. Her gown, a three-quarters dress of violet spider gauze over a cream satin petticoat, was stylish without being risqué. Diamonds sparkled at her throat.

"You know you always look good," he said. "Oh, before they come, I have something to tell you." He emptied his budget about Helen's doings with Bernard that afternoon. "Will you tell Dolmain?" he asked, when he had finished his tale.

Her anger with the father was no reason to let Helen fall into danger. There was no question of Dolmain's love of his daughter; he would certainly do what he should regarding her welfare. "He ought to know, yet I dislike to tattle on her. Yes, I expect I must tell him."

Dolmain and Lady Helen soon arrived. Caro could only assume he was a marvelous actor. The way he gazed at her, with a soft smile of admiration, was almost enough to make her question whether Newt was mistaken about her follower reporting to Curzon Street. She turned her attention to Helen, whom she had not had much opportunity to assess thus far. The girl was well turned out in a pale blue gown of sarsenet with a shawl of Albany gauze over her shoulders and a simple strand of pearls at her throat. She was pretty, but her smile was lukewarm.

"Good evening, Lady Winbourne," she said, dropping a small curtsey. Mr. Newton received an even smaller smile and curtsey.

"A great pleasure, Lady Helen," he said, bowing low, as if she were Queen Charlotte. "I have been looking forward to tonight. That is, to the ball. Standing up with you." He struggled through the greeting as if it were a bramble bush.

Lady Milchamp was also with them. She was an older lady, plump, smiling, and complacent, in a puce gown and satin turban with three short ostrich feathers. She had made her own debut thirty-odd years before, married, and removed to the country. It was not until the death of her husband ten years ago that she had returned to London for her own daughter's debut. She had bounced her bran-faced Amelia off with such stunning success (a marquess with twenty thousand a year) that she was much sought after to chaperon motherless debs. Lady Milchamp would accompany Newton and Lady Helen in Newt's carriage, leaving Dolmain and Caroline to use his rig. They all had a glass of wine, then left for Lady Sefton's ball.

"You are in high feather this evening, Caro," Dolmain said, when they were on their way in the carriage. "Very distinguished. I like that hairdo."

"Thank you, kind sir."

"We can drop in at Addie's later in the evening for a quick visit, if you like."

"I am not a veteran gambler," she said with a touch of asperity. "Everyone who matters will see me at Sefton's."

Dolmain stiffened at her curt reply. It sounded as if she was only going with him to reclaim her reputation. The drive continued a moment in silence. He had been looking forward to the evening, and wanted to clear the air. "Have I inadvertently done something to offend you, Caro?" he asked.

She would not charge him with having her followed, but she decided to mention Newton's discovery. "Newt saw your daughter today at Hyde Park," she said, and told the whole story.

"I am sure there is an innocent explanation," he replied. "Helen often mentions Bernard. She and Miss Blanchard help to raise funds for the French émigrés. Bernard is the secretary for the group. Very likely this woman they spoke of is some émigrée they are helping, now that I think of it. He could have called on Helen at home. He does not run tame there, but he is allowed to call on her, with Miss Blanchard present."

"I thought I ought to mention it," she said. His explanation jibed with what Newt had said, that it was not a romantic tryst.

"I appreciate your keeping an eye on Helen for me," he said warmly.

The ball achieved its aim of removing any shadow from Lady Winbourne's character, but it achieved nothing else. Caro was on pins and needles with Dolmain. Every word he uttered was examined for a second meaning. She tried to behave as if she cared for him, but human nature can only be pushed so far. Dolmain sensed her reserve, and was impatient with it, and her.

Newt's evening was even worse. It was plain as a pikestaff that Lady Helen had no use for him. She did not care much for horses, her speech was liberally peppered with French, and after standing up with him for the first set, she joined a younger group and ignored him until supper was served. When Newt and Helen joined Dolmain and Caroline at their table, further unpleasantness ensued.

Caroline made a few efforts to engage the chit in conversation, but received only monosyllabic replies. Yes, she had her court gown already prepared. When asked to describe it, she said only, "It is white silk."

This was a definite snub, and the other guests at their table knew it. Any deb could rave for hours over her presentation gown. Dolmain tried to cover her rudeness by making a joke about how much it had cost him, but it fell flat.

"You told Aunt Milchamp to do it up in style," his daughter snipped. "You know I would have preferred to give the money to charity, Papa. Comte Edouard de Lyons—so talented—is practically starving in a garret. Many of the aristos are suffering. Mama would prefer that the money be spent to ease their poverty and so do I. *Ça va sans dire.*"

"If Comte Edouard is still starving in a garret after being in the country for over two decades, it does not say much for his ambition," Dolmain retorted sharply.

Caroline sensed that this was an old argument between them. She was surprised that Helen spoke of her mother as if she were still alive, and that

Dolmain showed so little sympathy for his late wife's countrymen.

"He is a poet," Helen said, tossing her curls.

"How long does it take to dash off a sonnet?" Dolmain asked.

"He is writing a tragic epic poem on the revolution," Helen replied. "It takes years of research."

"A poet, eh?" Newton said, and stored up this nugget. He might turn his hand to scribbling up a poem, if that was what Lady Helen liked. And it would not take him two decades either.

When he expressed interest, Lady Helen condescended to inform him that the comte's epic was being written in the heroic style with rhymed couplets.

"I should like to read it, by Jove."

"It is in French, Mr. Newton," Helen said with a lift of her eyebrow. *"Vous ne parlez pas français, je crois?"*

"Eh? Daresay someone will translate it, if it is any good. They translated Homer and all those other foreigners."

"Good? It is superb. I have read it. I am the comte's sponsor. He will dedicate his epic to me."

"A good-looker, is he?" Newt asked.

"His face is ugly and his back is humped. It is his brain that is beautiful."

Having no luck with the lady, he turned his attention to the lobster patties instead and snabbled down half a dozen.

The evening was going so poorly that when Lady Helen announced she felt a migraine coming on, Caroline suggested they all leave. Caro and Dolmain left in his carriage while Newton had the ladies driven to Curzon Street.

"The evening is still young. Do you want to go to Addie's for an hour or so?" Dolmain asked.

"No, thank you, I would like to go home, but if

you want to play faro, you can go on after you let me off."

"I do not particularly want to play faro," he said through thin lips. "My hope was to provide some entertainment for you this evening. I have not seen any smiles so far."

To cover the true cause of her chagrin, she replied, "I take no pleasure in being snubbed by a schoolroom chit. If you hope to see Lady Helen make a suitable match, I suggest you teach her some manners."

"She is not usually rude. I don't know what ailed her this evening."

"Perhaps she shares the common misconception that I stole her necklace."

"I doubt it. And by the by, the necklace is not hers, it is mine, entailed on the estate. Caro, let us take a spin to settle your nerves."

In other words, he planned to take her to the infamous Hound and Hind again. Such a swell of fury rose up in her that she could no longer hold her tongue. "Why should *she* not think it, when you believe I am a thief? You had me followed, Lord Dolmain. Don't trouble to deny it. The carriage that was dogging me yesterday reported back to your house."

To his credit, he fought down the urge to deny it. "That was before I—we—before I knew you were innocent."

"You let me believe you were trying to draw the man out by that drive out the Chelsea Road last night. You knew all the time who he was. You lied to me. It was just an excuse to take me to that horrid place, the Hound and Hind."

"It is not a horrid place. Everyone goes there. It is perfectly discreet."

"Yes, discreet for men and their mistresses. If we had been seen, you know what people would have thought."

"I just wanted to be alone with you for a little while. I prevaricated because I felt badly about having hired Smith. I made the arrangement after visiting Lady Castlereagh that first morning. And no, I did not tell her I was doing it. There seemed some evidence that you—" She shot him a baleful glare. "Well, you were the only one who was actually sitting with Helen on that settee in the corner, just minutes before the diamonds disappeared. What was I to think? I called the man off last night when he reported to me."

"Kind of you!"

"So that is what has been bothering you all evening?"

"Yes, when a person I consider a friend sets a spy to dog my tail, I take it amiss. In my opinion, you would be better advised to set your spy to watching Pierre Bernard."

"How could he have taken it? He was not at the ball."

Caroline could think of no reply to this, so she resorted to a stony silence. She was still sulking when the carriage reached Berkeley Square. He accompanied her to her door.

"I am sorry the evening was not more enjoyable," he said. "Helen will apologize tomorrow. And I apologize now."

She gave one short, defiant look at him. "You have done your duty, Lord Dolmain. No one cut me dead this evening. I have not received any notes asking me to please stay away from future parties. In fact, Lady Jersey condescended to visit me this afternoon, so I assume that even Almack's has forgiven me. Your escort will no longer be necessary."

His eyes narrowed to angry slits, and his heart pounded hard. "Am I being given my congé, Lady Winbourne, now that I am of no further use to you?"

"If you choose to take it that way . . ."

"I don't. I refuse to believe you could be so cunning and underhanded and treacherous as to make love to me, only to achieve your own selfish ends. Tell me that is not what last night was all about."

She looked at him, with her mouth open in shock. He was accusing her of what he had done himself. "You dare to say that to me!" she exclaimed.

His tense face relaxed. An audible sigh of relief echoed on the air. "Forgive me that unconscionable piece of impertinence, if you can, Caro," he said, and lifted her hand to his lips. "You gave me quite a fright, my girl. I shall do myself the honor of calling on you again soon, after you have recovered from your little fit of temper. Until then, good evening, and thank you for . . . last night."

He bowed and strode back to his carriage. Caroline went into the house, nodded to Crumm, and went straight up to her bedchamber. Georgiana had already retired. Caro sat on the side of the bed, reliving those last moments before Dolmain departed. He had seemed genuinely concerned, and wonderfully worried at the possibility that she did not care for him. Was it possible she was mistaken, that he truly cared for her? Suspicion did point to her; there was no denying that. Was it so bad that he had hired a man to follow her? He had called off the man now, and apologized.

Her anger melted away. But as she lay in bed, she knew that nothing could be settled until the necklace was found. Society had been coerced into pretending to believe her innocent, but Lady Helen's rudeness had raised doubts again. The notion had been growing that Helen had stolen her own necklace, hidden it somewhere, and told her papa it was stolen, but the girl's cold behavior that evening suggested that she thought Caroline had it. What other reason could Helen have for being cold and rude to her? The girl would have been acting guilty if she had taken it herself. No, someone else had it, and she had to find it.

Chapter Eleven

Caroline was tempted to refuse Lady Helen's invitation that arrived the next morning, for she sensed that Dolmain had forced her to write it. Helen apologized for her fit of the sulks the evening before, blaming it on her migraine. She asked if Lady Winbourne would do her the honor of accompanying her on a drive that afternoon. Curiosity and a hope to learn more about Pierre Bernard inclined Caroline to accept. She suspected Dolmain was trying to confirm in the public eye that she was on intimate terms with his family, and was pleased with him. When Newton arrived and expressed the keenest interest in the trip, she wrote back accepting the offer.

Dolmain's stately crested city carriage duly arrived at the door at three—his best carriage. Was this a compliment to her, or to his daughter? Lady Helen did not condescend to alight, but sent her footman to summon Lady Winbourne, who was highly incensed at this piece of impertinence.

"Rag-mannered! I am tempted to say I have changed my mind," said Caroline, her eyes flashing dangerously.

Newt's reply was to hand her her bonnet. "Cutting up your nose to spite your face. You might discover something. I could not get word one out of her last night."

Caroline arranged her fashionable high poke bonnet with a cascade of curled feathers falling over the brim and said, "If she says one rude thing, I shall give her a piece of my mind."

"She won't," Newton assured her, on what evidence, even Caro could not imagine. As they left the house, he said, "There is a day for you. Not a sky in the clouds."

Glancing up, she saw that he had inadvertently given a correct description. London was blanketed by a solid gray cloud with no patch of blue visible.

It was soon clear that Dolmain had spoken severely to his daughter. Helen smiled and offered her hand, covered in a dainty blue kid glove, to them both. "It is very kind of you to join me, Lady Winbourne," she said, while her sharp eyes trotted from Caroline's stylish bonnet to her equally elegant violet walking suit. "I thought we might visit Bond Street. Where did you buy that bonnet? It has a French look to it."

"At Madame Lanctot's, on Bond Street. I should be happy to accompany you."

It was hardly an outing to suit Newt, but he said, "Lanctot's it is." He then steeled himself to peer at Lady Helen and said, "Yours is nice, too—your bonnet."

She inclined her head gracefully. "*Merci*, Mr. Newton."

"*Pass doo toot.*"

Conversation was stilted during the drive to Bond Street. Once the occupants descended to stroll along the street, the shop windows provided easier conversation. Lady Helen bought a painted muslin fan bearing a picture of the Ponte Vecchio. They stopped at Lanctot's, where she tried on a dozen bonnets of a style much too sophisticated for her. Newton's ingenuity was stretched to the limit to vary his compliments on them all, and Caroline's to let the girl know they did not suit her, without sounding like a shrew. Lady Helen did not buy a bonnet, but it was not due to Caroline's advice.

"They are much too dear," she said in a quiet aside. "Five guineas for a bonnet! *C'est incroyable!*" This seemed a strange objection for one of the Season's greatest heiresses, until she added, "Imagine how much food that would buy for the émigrés."

"Comte Edouard could dash off a few stanzas on that, I wager," Newton said supportively, and actually won a smile. Or bought one, for Helen soon followed up by selling him six tickets to a fair for the émigrés.

Newton had some reason to assume he was finding favor with the charmer. Helen did most of her talking to him. Caroline was struck by a different idea; Helen did not want to converse with her. Her papa had ordered her to be polite, but friendship cannot be commanded.

When they passed a small jewelry shop, Helen said, "Would you mind stopping in here a moment? I brought a brooch with me. The pin is loose and has to be repaired before I wear it."

Newton interjected a note of discord by saying, "Was the lock of your diamond necklace loose, by any chance?"

"No, Papa had just had it looked at," she replied. It was the first time the subject of the necklace had arisen.

Caroline was determined to follow up this lead, despite the girl's obvious distaste for the subject. "It was a terrible and shocking thing to lose it. I do hope it was insured?"

Lady Helen turned to her. "No, it had sat in Papa's safe for years. As it was not worn, he did not have it insured." She turned away immediately, but while she spoke, she looked Caroline directly in the eye with no sign of wavering.

They went into the shop. While Caroline examined a simple day brooch done in citrine and marcasite, Helen opened her reticule and drew out a handkerchief edged in ecru lace. She gasped, and exclaimed in a stricken voice, "It is gone! My emerald brooch is missing!"

Caroline felt as if she had been kicked in the stomach by a mule. Not again! Their eyes met. Helen did not look guiltily away, but said in heartfelt accents, "Oh, pray do not look at me like that, Lady Winbourne. I know you did not take it. My reticule must have fallen open at Madame Lanctot's. Let us return at once and see if she has put it away for me."

"It may have fallen out of the handkerchief," Caroline said. It seemed odd that such an obvious thing had not occurred to the girl—almost as if she knew the brooch was not there.

Lady Helen rifled through her reticule. "I had it in my handkerchief. It must have fallen out. No, it is not here."

"Let us go to Lanctot's, at once," Caroline said, and they all rushed out of the shop, back to the milliner's.

Helen spoke to Madame in French, showing her the reticule and the empty handkerchief. Madame shook her head firmly. *"Mais non. L'épingle n'est pas ici. Vous n'avez pas ouvert la sac à main ici, mademoiselle."*

Helen turned to look at Caroline. There was no accusation in her eyes, but a definite air of slyness. Caroline was morally certain the brooch was not stolen, but had been put aside by Helen. And if she was prevaricating now, then very likely she also knew what had happened to the necklace.

"It must have fallen out on the street," Newton said. "Let us retrace our steps."

"Or it might be in the carriage," Lady Helen said, leaping on other possibilities. She turned to Caroline and said with a dramatic air worthy of Mrs. Siddons, "I don't know *what* Papa will say. The brooch belonged to Mama."

"You should notify him at once if you don't find

it," Caroline said. She had no rational reason for wanting Dolmain to be apprised of it immediately. It loomed like a trip to the tooth drawer as an unpleasant thing that must be done, and the sooner it was over, the better.

They retraced their steps, discovering no sign of the brooch. They then hailed the carriage, which had been driving alongside them, and searched it, also in vain.

"Let us go to Berkeley Square and write a note to your papa," Caroline suggested. She wanted to be present to hear how Helen explained the loss of the brooch to him.

As the carriage bowled along, Helen became quite voluble. "The brooch was not that valuable," she said, addressing herself to Caroline now, quite ignoring Newton. "The stones were quite small, but Papa values it highly. He gave it to Mama as an engagement gift, and anything of hers is sacred to him, you must know. He loved her so very much. There has never been any other woman for him. There never will be. She was extremely beautiful. It pains him so to speak of her death that he never lets us discuss her at home, but we have her portrait, made up into a sort of shrine. There are always fresh flowers beneath it. Mama loved roses. It was a great love affair. His parents forbade the match, but he would not heed them."

Caroline listened to this outburst with avid interest. Obviously this was why Dolmain had never remarried. The question was, was he still in love with his dead wife? What chance had she against a ghost, who would never do any wrong, never lose her temper, but live forever green in memory? Even if he married her, would she take second place to a ghost?

Helen was looking at her expectantly. To break the silence, Caro said, "I know how he feels. I still

101

treasure the golden locket my husband gave me as an engagement token."

"You certainly don't hesitate to talk about Julian. You never shut up about him," Newton reminded her.

"Lady Winbourne is an outgoing sort," Helen said. "What we call in French a lady of *esprit*. Papa keeps things all pent up inside, but he feels very deeply. He showed me the house in Brighton where Mama lived when he was courting her. It is a modest cottage on Bartholomew Avenue, around the corner from the Town Hall. Papa bought it for Mama. She gave it to a cousin after their marriage. It is still used by the émigrés."

Lady Winbourne listened with interest to all of this, thinking how shattered Dolmain must have been when his wife died. She had been shattered at Julian's death, too, but now she felt ready to go on with her life. Why could not he?

Helen ran on with other details of her mama. "I was named after her. My name is actually Marie-Hélène. Mama was called Marie, so she called me Hélène. Englishmen cannot pronounce it properly," she said, "and even on my birth certificate it was written as Helen."

This sudden spate of confidences was unlike Lady Helen. It occurred to Caroline that the girl was rattling on with this ancient history to prevent talk of how the brooch had got lost.

She cut into the story. "Are you certain you had the brooch when you left home, Lady Helen?"

"Miss Blanchard did not take it, if that is what you are implying," the girl shot back angrily.

"No one is accusing her." How quickly she leapt to Blanchard's defense! "I meant you might have left it at home."

"No," Helen said, settling down. "I looked in my reticule last thing before I left the house. I do not plan to involve you in this, Lady Winbourne. I know Papa will agree with me that we must keep this *entre nous*, in case of gossip. We both feel very badly that you were drawn into the other affair."

Keeping it quiet might prevent more gossip, but it did not solve the matter. As soon as they reached Berkeley Square, Lady Helen wrote her note and dispatched it to the Horse Guards. Caroline expected Dolmain to come bolting at once, but they sat an hour before he arrived. Everyone's nerves were stretched to the breaking point. Georgiana sat with them; she had been told the story but had little to say about it. She just looked at Caroline and shook her head ruefully, as if to say, "You have done it again."

As soon as Dolmain entered the saloon, Helen rose, burst into tears, and ran to pitch herself into his arms. "I am sorry, Papa! I don't know how it happened, but Lady Winbourne did not steal it this ti— did not take it. My reticule never left my hand." She then fell, sobbing, on his neck.

Caroline sat like a kettle on a slow boil, growing hotter by the moment. *Did not steal it this time* was what Helen had meant. It was as good as saying they believed she had stolen the necklace.

Dolmain comforted his daughter, while looking at Caro apologetically. "There, there," he said. "It is no great loss."

Helen lifted her moist eyes and said in hushed accents, "But it was *hers*, Papa. You must be *devastated*."

"It is a pity, but you have plenty of other mementoes."

He drew Helen's arms from around his neck and took a seat. His daughter sat on the floor, curled up at his feet like a puppy, with her head resting against his knees.

"We shan't bruit this one about town," he said to Caroline. "I had hoped to foster a friendship between you and my daughter, but I fear I have only caused further mischief."

Caroline noticed that Helen's tears were drying. Her mask of chagrin was transformed into a sly, satisfied smile.

"Lady Winbourne and I got along splendidly, Papa," she said, smiling up at him. "I like her excessively."

Caro sat like a stone. She had an odd way of showing it! What a consummate liar the girl was.

"Well, that is something," Dolmain said. It was clear to Caroline that, whatever about the brooch, he valued his cunning rogue of a daughter above rubies and believed every lie she uttered. "That being the case, let us all go out together this evening," he suggested.

Helen's smile faded, then her pretty little face hardened to anger. But when her father looked down at her, she put on a smile and said, "How lovely. I would like it of all things. Let us all go to Aunt Miriam's rout together."

"I have made other plans for the evening," Caroline said, with a long, cold look at Helen. *Find someone else to blame the loss of your jewels on,* that look said.

Dolmain stared at her in dismay. In his innocence, he thought his plan of sending the ladies out together had succeeded admirably. It was unfortunate about the little brooch—a strange coincidence, but Helen had gone a mile out of her way to make clear Caro had not taken it. He would quiz Helen more thoroughly when they were alone. It was demmed odd that Caro had been present both times. . . . She would hardly dare to cadge another piece of jewelry. Surely she had not taken the necklace? But then, why did she refuse to accompany them? "Your escort will no longer be necessary," she had said last night. Was the hussy leading him a merry chase?

"I am sorry to hear it," he said, forcing himself to maintain civility. "Go and get your bonnet, Helen. We have taken enough of Lady Winbourne's time."

Helen hopped up with the greatest alacrity. She thanked Lady Winbourne effusively for a lovely afternoon, and even remembered to nod to Georgiana and Newton before leaving.

When they had gone, Caroline said, "What do you make of that, Georgie?"

"The chit is a conning rogue," Georgiana replied. "She as well as said she thinks you took the necklace. I know you noticed it, for your face froze like ice when she said, 'Lady Winbourne did not steal it this time,' or practically said it."

"Nothing of the sort," Newton objected. "Said as plain as day Caro didn't take it. You wasn't listening, Georgie."

"I was listening with my heart," Georgie replied. "That girl dislikes you, Caro. What is more, she fears you."

"With good reason."

Newt's jaw dropped an inch. "You never mean you did steal the trumpery thing!"

"Of course not! She has it herself, hidden away somewhere. And I mean to find out what she is up to. She nearly leapt down my throat when I asked if she was sure she had not left the brooch home. She assured me that Miss Blanchard had not taken it. Now, that is odd, you must own, to go defending the woman when no one had accused her, or even mentioned her name."

"Don't forget Bernard," Newton said. "It is pretty clear the pair of them are preying on poor little Helen."

Georgiana and Caro exchanged a look that spoke volumes.

Lady Helen drove home with her papa while the groom took the other carriage to the stable.

Dolmain was reluctant to cast aspersions on Caro, even indirectly, but it was beginning to seem the charmer was nothing else but a conniving thief, using her beauty to disarm suspicion. He felt a deep aching need when he remembered their drive to the Hound and Hind.

"When you were walking, Helen, what did you do with your reticule? Which hand did you hold it in?" he asked.

"In my left hand, as I always do. Mr. Newton was on my right side. I know you like Lady Winbourne, Papa, but I hope you will not make me go out with her again. I had a horrid time."

"Did anything else unpleasant occur, other than losing the brooch?" he asked, instantly wary.

"She had something horrid to say about every bonnet I tried on. Do you know, Papa, I just remembered that when I was trying on bonnets at Lanctot's, I set my reticule on the counter beside Lady Winbourne. But I am sure she would not steal—would she?" She turned her innocent eyes on him.

"No, of course not," he said mechanically. But who else could have taken it? It was just as well Lady Winbourne had refused his invitation that evening. He could not go on seeing her. He was too easily led into folly by her. If she was innocent, he had done what he could to defend her name; and if she was guilty, then he had been very foolish to lift a finger in her defense. And a complete ass to fall in love with her. His heart felt like a ton of lead in his chest.

He fell into a morose mood for the remainder of the drive home, gazing out the carriage window. In an effort to stifle the pain of Caro's treachery, he tried to think of how he could solve this mess, once and for all. He had put out word to all jewelers to call Bow Street if anyone tried to sell the necklace. He had sent word out on the grapevine that there was a reward of ten thousand pounds if it ended up at Stop Hole Abbey, where stolen jewels were fenced. The necklace was worth three times that, to say nothing of the emotional value.

He did not even glance at Helen again, or notice the triumphant smile lifting her lips, as she slid her little gloved hand trustingly into his.

Chapter Twelve

Caroline was gratified to receive enough invitations in the afternoon post to show that society had not rejected her. If rumors of this latest loss got about, however—and they might despite Helen's assurance that it would be kept quiet—then her situation would rapidly worsen. Every dog has one bite, but the second nip will ofttimes prove fatal—to the dog. It was of the utmost importance that she not only solve the mystery of the missing jewels, but also be seen at the most haute of ton parties, such as Lady Marlborough's ball that evening.

The ever-faithful Newton would accompany her, after taking his dinner at Berkeley Square. They did not discuss the thefts over dinner with the servants about, but as soon as Newton brought his port to the Gold Saloon, Caro said, "It is pretty clear that the necklace was never stolen at all. I am now convinced Helen carried it home in her reticule and passed it on to someone. Miss Blanchard is the obvious person."

"And Bernard is in it up to his neck," Newt added. "He is the one getting money to bring that girl to London."

"The money comes from selling the necklace," Georgie said.

Newton scowled. "They are fleecing the poor girl, preying on her innocence. Demmed shame. She wouldn't hurt a flea."

There was no arguing with a man in love. "Who could this girl be?" Caroline asked.

Georgie replied, "You really should have gone to the ball with Dolmain and Lady Helen tonight, Caro. I understand your feelings, but how will you discover anything about Miss Blanchard if you lose contact with them?"

"I could try to get a line on Bernard," Newt offered.

"Yes, and we must have someone follow Miss Blanchard as well," Caroline added. "I wager she will be running that emerald brooch off to Stop Hole Abbey this very day."

Newt peered owlishly into the grate. "They'll wait until dark. Bernard will go. A lady wouldn't venture to the Abbey."

Caro said, "As we do not know where to find Bernard, we must keep track of Miss Blanchard. Crumm will find me a man for the job. He was useful to Julian for such things in the past."

She called Crumm into the saloon and told him what she required. He pulled pensively at the lobe of his misshapen ear, and after listening, said, "Nolly Norton would be the lad for the job, but alas, he is a guest of the king at the moment. Newgate. Caught dead to rights nabbing a cove's purse. When all is said and done, 'tis best to keep such matters in the fambly. I'll go myself, and let young Roger answer the door. His head will be so big, he'll scarcely be able to carry it, but I'll fix that in short order when I come back." Young Roger, the first footman, was a decade older than Crumm, but half his size.

"Thank you, Crumm. I knew I might count on you," Caroline said. "But you are rather . . . er, large. Can you loiter near Dolmain's house without looking suspicious?"

"No need. I will hire a hackney coach for the night—Ned Stork has a fast team—and tool it around the block. No one will notice a dark hackney at night. She'll not get away, madam. You may count on Crumm." His massive shoulders squared and his chin rose to an impressive angle at this speech.

"I depend on you. There will be the usual pourboire," she added, which brought a light to Crumm's sharp eyes. The wages at Berkeley Square were good, but pourboires had been rare since his lordship's demise, as were such sprees as this.

"I had best be off at once. I have a few preparations to make," he said, and left.

After Lady Georgiana's first taste of life the afternoon she had accompanied Caroline to the Pantheon Bazaar, she had felt an urge for more excitement. She did not foresee much hope for it at Lady Marlborough's ball, however, so she meant to spend her evening with her customary company, a novel and a bottle of Madeira, in the small parlor. She was not left completely out of things. If Crumm returned with important news, she was to send a note to the ball informing Caroline that she was ill, to make an excuse for Caro and Newton to leave early.

"My old complaint, a reaction to shellfish," she said.

At the ball, Caroline had the satisfaction of her usual popularity. To be on Lady Marlborough's guest list was as good a character reference as any lady required. Lord Alton pursued her quite openly, and asked her to drive out the next afternoon. When Silence Jersey asked her in a coy way where Dolmain was this evening, she could reply with an air suggesting intimacy that Lady Helen had mentioned they felt obliged to attend her aunt Miriam's rout.

"I heard you and Helen were on the strut today."

"Yes," Caro said, forcing a smile. She added, at random, that Helen and her papa would likely drop in at Lady Marlborough's later. After she said it, she realized they might do just that—and God only knew how Dolmain would behave toward her. Helen might very well have succeeded in turning him against her.

With this possibility in mind, she accepted a second dance with Lord Alton, to give society something different to gossip about. They were just finishing the cotillion when Dolmain and Helen entered, around eleven-thirty. Caroline had been keeping watch on the doorway, and saw them come in. How handsome he looked in his formal evening clothes! The fluttering of her heart increased when his dark eyes raked the floor. When he spotted her, he stared, not smiling, but just looking coolly. She gazed back, unable to look away.

Dolmain's thoughts were far from cool. He felt a burning sensation inside that had nothing to do with diamonds or emeralds, to see Caro flirting with Alton. It had been so long since he had experienced jealousy that he scarcely recognized it. The emotion had been long obliterated from his marriage by the time Marie finally decamped on him. His major sensation at the time had been relief, quickly followed by shame. His violent passion for his wife had not survived six months. That soon he had discovered her only love had been for his wealth and his title, in that order. But for a few months he had endured agonies of jealousy.

Although Caro did not resemble Marie physically, there was something of the same vivacity and coquetry in her manner. She exercised the same heady power over him. A lively lady was always his weakness. He had no use for dull virtue, but there must be virtue in a wife. He had learned that lesson at great cost. No shadow had been cast on Lady Winbourne's chastity when her husband was alive. That was not her weakness. When she loved, she loved only one man. But had she other, secret

111

vices? An echo whispered in his ear. *We all have our little secret vices, you must know.* She had told him so herself.

When the cotillion ended, he looked to see that Helen had found a partner, then hastened across the floor to claim Caro.

"Lady Winbourne," he said with a bow.

She was so relieved at his continuing patronage that she greeted him warmly, despite having sunk to "Lady Winbourne."

Alton held on to her arm and viewed Dolmain with a jealous eye. "Tomorrow afternoon, then, Lady Winbourne?" he asked.

"Around four," she agreed, happy to show Dolmain he was not master of the field.

"As we have had our two dances, I must leave you to Dolmain. I look forward to tomorrow." He lifted her fingers to his lips, kissed the air an inch above them, bowed, and left.

"Two dances!" Dolmain exclaimed, with an accusing glance. "That suggests a certain intimacy with the gentleman. Determined to set society's collective tongue wagging one way or the other, eh, Caro?"

"Alton is an old friend," she replied, pleased at his ill humor. "You must not blame me for society's love of scandal." Not wishing to make a point of it, she immediately spoke of other things. "How was your aunt's rout party?"

"Tedious. Orgeat and macaroons, a fiddler and a piano player, and not a pretty lady in the room, barring Helen." Certainly no one to touch this violet-eyed charmer. "I was the youngest gent there, and we have already agreed I am ancient."

"How boring for your daughter."

"Not at all. Her job was to ingratiate Miriam, who is seventy-five years old, and a spinster. In other words, her fortune is at liberty. Odd you do not pity me."

"What lady would you prefer to gaze on than Helen?"

"You—the fairest of them all." He bowed and reached for her hand as he spoke. The orchestra was taking an intermission. As the crowd surged toward the refreshment parlor, Caro and Dolmain moved to the side of the room and sat down.

"Lady Helen will have need of her aunt's fortune if she continues scattering her jewelry about town in her present fashion," Caro said, to get the matter out in the open.

He sighed wearily. "Let us speak of other things."

"No, Dolmain. I am not much good at walking on eggs. Let us speak of what is on both our minds. I did not take either the necklace or the brooch." She took a deep breath and continued, "In fact, I do not see how anyone could have taken them. I think your daughter took them herself."

He stared at her as if she had accused Helen of murder.

"Don't look at me like that!" she said crossly. "No one had access to them except Helen and myself. I suspect your daughter is running some rig. She is young; she would not realize the seriousness of what she is doing. I believe Miss Blanchard is involved, and her cousin, Bernard." She gave her reasons, mentioning the girl Helen wanted to see in London, and her defense of Miss Blanchard when no one had accused her.

"This is ludicrous!" Dolmain said angrily. "Helen knows the difference between right and wrong. Everyone who knows her will tell you her character is above reproach."

Yet as he looked at Caro's pale, worried face, he found it equally ludicrous to believe that she was a thief. He was in the unenviable position of having to choose between believing his daughter, whom he loved more than anyone else in the world, and the

113

lady he was fast discovering he loved nearly as much.

"In a case like this, no one involved should be above suspicion. You did not hesitate to have me followed," she retorted. "Who is this Miss Blanchard? What do you actually know about her?"

"She came with excellent references. She taught the Duke of Halford's daughters. Her influence on Helen has been excellent. Helen has blossomed under her care. She would never harm the girl."

"She has not harmed Helen. She has stolen valuable items belonging to you. It is myself she has harmed—my reputation."

"Alton does not appear to mind your reputation," he shot back, and felt like a schoolboy for his childish outburst.

"Don't try to change the subject. Do you refuse to question Miss Blanchard, to look into her associates?"

"You are not accusing only Miss Blanchard, Lady Winbourne," he said coldly. "You are also accusing my daughter of duplicity. It is irresponsible of you to do so. I assure you Helen would never behave in such an underhanded manner. We are very close. If she had fallen into a hobble, she would not hesitate a moment to ask me for money."

"That would depend on what she required it for, I think."

His eyes darkened to jet. A dangerous glint of fury flashed from their depths. His rigid lips lent a curt edge to his voice. "What are you suggesting, madam? That she has murdered someone? That she has gambled away her fortune? That she has fallen prey to a gazetted fortune hunter and is robbing her own father to oblige him? She has not been in London above a week. She is carefully chaperoned at all times."

"She was not so carefully chaperoned the night she went to the Pantheon!" Caroline retaliated. "Is

Pierre Bernard also above suspicion because he claims to be a cousin of your governess? Is that sufficient for you? I am the daughter of a respected clergyman. My character is also good."

"You are not so innocent as a seventeen-year-old lady."

"I rather think I am a good deal more innocent."

"This is pointless. We have nothing further to say to each other. Good evening, madam."

He rose, performed a stiff bow, and walked away at a gait that betrayed anger. Caroline was emotionally exhausted. She wanted only to go home, and looked around for Newton. Sally Jersey came surging forward, her tongue running like a brook.

"Naughty puss!" she said. "You have annoyed Dolmain by giving Lord Alton two dances. It is your affair, but if I were you, I would prefer Dolmain. A marquess after all, and with those lovely estates in Kent and Derbyshire. Alton has only the one, you must know, and he *hires* his town house. You must not let Lady Helen put you off with her freakish sentiment for the Frenchies. She will be bounced off this Season. So pretty, and a handsome dot. You will not have her on your hands if you take Dolmain." She peered inquisitively for her victim's response.

Caroline forced herself to answer in kind. "You are too ridiculous. I have not had an offer from either one of them."

"So standing up twice with Alton was a ploy to bring Dolmain up to scratch! You are up to all the rigs, Caro."

She darted off before Caroline could deny this charge. Newton came wandering forward, looking remarkably like a badger walking on his hind legs and wearing a red wig.

"No word from Georgie?" he asked, sitting beside her.

"No, but I should like to leave now."

"Haven't had a dance with Lady Helen yet. Daresay her card is full by now. Meant to tell her I am writing a poem."

This unlikely statement diverted Caro. "You, writing a poem? Pray, what is it about, Newt?"

"King Arthur," he replied so promptly that she knew he was actually trying his hand at poesy. "Mean to say, an epic. Can't write an epic about mad old King George, nor Prinny. Has to be heroic or about a great action achieved by a hero. Read it in Dr. Johnson's *Dictionary*. Comte Edouard is already doing the revolution in France. King Arthur has King Louis beat all hollow, the round table and knights and all."

"To be sure. Very lively stuff."

"Just give me a minute. If Helen's card is full, I shall go with you and get at the epic. I'll just mention my epic poem to her, see what she has to say."

He was back in five minutes. "Called for the rig," he said. "Her card is full. Might have known. She thought the epic a dandy idea. Said something about *Le Morte d'Arthur*. Sounds French. King Arthur wasn't a Frenchie, was he?"

"No. I believe some Frenchman wrote a poem about him."

"You mean it's already been done!" he exclaimed.

"Not recently. You could update it. Shall we go now?"

"Already been done, eh?" he said, his outrage dwindling to a smile. "That simplifies things. I'll have a look at this *Morte d'Arthur* to refresh my memory. I know there is a round table in there somewhere."

Caroline was just looking for her hostess when Lady Marlborough came hastening forward, a frown on her kindly face. "A note from Lady Georgiana, Caroline. I hope it is not bad news."

Caroline took it and scanned it. "She has taken ill. She should not have eaten that lobster, but she

116

does love it so. I had best go home. A lovely ball, Lady Marlborough."

"Thank you. My best to Lady Georgiana. I shall tell Dolmain you left. He will be sorry he missed a dance with you."

"Thank you," Caroline said weakly, and escaped.

The carriage rattled along for a few blocks. Newton stuck his head out the window and said, "He's following you again."

"Who is?"

"Mr. Smith. He has changed one horse and the carriage to try to fool us. I would recognize that bay with the white stockings anywhere. I thought Dolmain called off his man."

"It seems he has called him back on," Caro said grimly. There was no deceiving Newt where horses were concerned. All her vague regrets hardened to anger. "I knew he did not trust me. Helen got to work on her papa as soon as they left Berkeley Square this afternoon. She convinced him I stole that brooch."

"If she convinced him, then someone convinced her."

"She is not the innocent you take her for, Newt. She is as skilled as a professional actress. All that childish display of pitching herself into Papa's arms in tears, sitting at his feet like a puppy, and all the while she was a scheming sneak."

Yet Dolmain had seemed friendly when he first arrived at Marlborough's ball. It was only after she accused Helen of stealing her own jewelry that he stiffened up. Perhaps she should not have done it. A father was bound to stick up for his own flesh and blood. But she still felt in her bones that Lady Helen was behind the whole affair. And furthermore, Dolmain had already set his man to follow her when he was flattering her, telling her she was the fairest of them all. That carriage must have fol-

117

lowed her from Berkeley Square. She had not told Dolmain where she meant to go this evening.

"Can you not have John Groom speed the team up? I hope Crumm has discovered something interesting."

Chapter Thirteen

Crumm was back on duty at the door when Caroline and Newton arrived at Berkeley Square.

"What is it, Crumm? What did you learn?" she asked eagerly, before she had crossed the threshold.

"Ye'd best have a glass of wine, your ladyship."

"Good God, what is it?" she exclaimed, her eyes wide in fear. It was not like Crumm to make a mountain of a molehill.

"I'll get the wine," Newton said, and led her into the saloon, where Georgie was sitting, pale and shaken.

"You've heard?" Georgie asked.

Crumm rushed forward to prevent Lady Georgiana from stealing his thunder. "That Miss Blanchard mort you asked me to keep an eye out for—she's been done."

"Done what?" Caroline asked in confusion.

"Done in," Newt translated. "Dead. Ain't that it, Crumm?"

"It is, sir." In the excitement of the moment Crumm forgot himself and poured three glasses of wine. Georgie already held a glass of Madeira. He took a sip before commencing his tale.

Caroline felt a strange whistling sound in her ears. Miss Blanchard was dead, her chief suspect murdered. How was anything to be solved without her to follow or question?

"How did it happen? Who did it?" she asked.

Crumm shook his head in apology. "There was no

getting a peep at the cove at all, milady. I was stationed at the corner in Ned Stork's plain black rattler with one eye on the front door of the ken and one on the road."

"He means he was in a hackney, keeping an eye on the house," Newt interpolated.

Crumm continued, "Aye, that's it. The door opened at half past nine. The malkin you described to me come out, leading a dog on a leash—to do his nightly business, I figured. Odd they would choose a lady for the job, but there was a footman with her. They headed south, toward Piccadilly. At the corner, she sent the lad back. I went along after her on foot, with the rattler and prads coming behind me. If she got into a rig, I'd need the rattler to follow her. She looked behind her, nervous-like, but not so frightened she turned tail and went home. I lost sight of her when she turned the corner. Before I reached her, I heard the shot. I went flying for'ard, but there was neither man nor boy to be seen, only the old lady laying in the road, and a rig flying away like old Nick was after him.

"Not knowing for sure the shot came from the rig, I let the dog go, thinking he'd have the wits to go after whoever done it. The unnatural animal just set there, letting out a mighty howling. I stopped to see if I could get a word out of her, but she was past it. I called for Ned and hopped into the rattler. We chased t'other rig, but it got away from us. It turned right at Tiburn Lane, heading out of town. There was nothing to tell it from a hundred other rattlers in town."

Newt, who had been listening with complete absorption, said, "Did you notice the nags?"

"Only that they was darkish, big fellows. One had a blaze on the forehead, like half the prads in England."

Georgie said. "I wonder if Miss Blanchard was just walking the dog, or was she meeting someone.

Her sending the footman back looks as if she wished to be alone, does it not?"

"Did you just leave Miss Blanchard lying in the road, dead?" Caroline asked Crumm.

"Nay, I have more respect for a corpse. I didn't want her coming back to haunt me. I wrote up a note giving Blanchard's name and address and all, and had it delivered to Bow Street by a linkboy. A Runner will be sent off to Curzon Street. But I am getting ahead of myself. Before I left the scene, there was already a footman scuttling out of the house nearest to the body. She'll be took care of prompt-like, never fear."

A frisson scuttled up Caroline's spine to think of the poor woman lying on the cold ground. "God only knows how long it will take Bow Street to handle the matter. We should notify the servants at Dolmain's house at once," she said. "They must be worrying that Miss Blanchard has not returned. Helen will be dreadfully upset," she said, speaking distractedly.

Newton had a different worry. "Let us hope no one saw you, Crumm, or they'll report that you killed her."

Crumm spared him a tolerant glance. "What they saw, if they saw anything in the dark, was an elderly country gent in a fustian coat, with white hair pulled into a tail. I didn't come down in the last rain. I've been on the earth a few years."

Georgiana said, "I scarcely recognized Crumm myself when he came in. He gave me quite a start."

"I never left the house all evening, as her ladyship can testify," Crumm added, with a commanding look at Georgiana.

Georgie felt again that excitement that sent her heart racing. But when she spoke, she said calmly, "Quite right, Crumm—but I hope I am not obliged to repeat that plumper under oath. I cannot like the thought of perjuring myself."

121

"You soon get used to it," he assured her. "Nay, don't faint, your ladyship. They'll take a gentry mort's word for it without using the oath book."

Caroline and Newt asked Crumm a dozen questions, but no new information was forthcoming. The next matter was: What should they do about it? The murder had been reported to Bow Street, who would notify Curzon Street. The servants there would see that Dolmain was informed. There was nothing more they could do except wait and worry—especially worry.

It now seemed clear that Miss Blanchard was involved with some dangerous criminals, and it looked very much as if she had managed to involve Lady Helen as well. It was no longer just a matter of stealing. Now Helen would have to tell what she knew.

"You have certainly done your job well, Crumm," Caro said.

"That ain't the whole of it," Crumm said, with a wise look that promised trouble.

"Good Lord, there's more?" Newt said in a choked voice.

Crumm's hand went into his pocket and came out. He held his closed fist out to Caroline and slowly opened the fingers to reveal the missing emerald brooch. "I did a quick search when I seen she was dead, thinking there might be a note in her pocket, which there weren't, nor in her reticule either. I never touched the guinea and two shillings and three pennies, though it wouldn't surprise me much if the Runner pockets them. I just took this set o' sparklers, which was wrapped up in a handkerchee. I have the handkerchee as well," he said, and fished it out of his other pocket. It was a delicate linen square, edged in ecru lace, an exact replica of the one Lady Helen had held when she announced the brooch was missing.

Caroline was overcome with a feeling of nausea.

"So Helen did give the brooch to Miss Blanchard," she said.

"Rubbish!" Newt replied angrily. "Proves Blanchard stole it out of her reticule. That's Lady Helen's handkerchief."

"Helen said she had the brooch when she left home. She made a point of saying Miss Blanchard had not stolen it."

Shoved to the corner, Newton said, "That's as may be, but there must be a good reason for it."

Georgie cleared her throat and said in a nervous voice, "You had best hide the brooch, Caro. There is not much point my pretending Crumm was here all evening if Bow Street should come pouncing in and find the stolen brooch in his possession."

Caro looked alarmed and handed it back to Crumm. Crumm handed it to Newt, who smiled gently. "I'll give it back to her," he said. "Bound to soften her up, a memento of her mama."

"Don't be a fool, man!" Crumm said, and snatched the brooch back. "Who will believe you didn't snaffle it when you're found in possession?"

"It should be returned, though," Caroline said. She wished Crumm had left it in Miss Blanchard's pocket. That would have exonerated her in the second theft at least. In any case, his finding it on Miss Blanchard was proof of her involvement. She could not be the moving force, though, or she would not now be dead. She was a pawn. The king was still at large.

"Do you think it possible Miss Blanchard was shot by an ordinary robber, Crumm?" she asked.

"I never seen a prigger yet that left his victim's purse in his pocket—to say nothing of the green sparklers. The mort had a meeting planned, or why did she send the footman off?"

"Crumm is right, Caro," Georgie said. "She might have been meeting the man to give him the brooch."

"That makes sense. If only we knew who he is. Bernard?"

"Would Miss Blanchard's cousin murder her?" Georgie said.

"If he is her cousin," Newt said.

"I knew a jarkman as killed his own pa," Crumm announced. "He was up for being a vagrant. Figured the judge might go easy on a orphan."

"This is impossible!" Caroline said. "There are too many mysteries. I have half a mind to tell Dolmain the whole." But when she remembered his cold stare and the odious way he had called her madam, she shrank from confronting him. He would think she had stolen the brooch—and probably killed Miss Blanchard into the bargain, since she had left the ball early.

"What are you going to do about the brooch?" Georgie asked.

Four pairs of eyes turned to the brooch, which had found its way to the sofa table, where it gleamed malignly.

"Thing to do," Newt said, "take it back."

"Back where?" Georgie asked.

"Where Blanchard was shot. Let Bow Street find it."

Caro caught the gleam of interest in Crumm's criminal eye and said, "Someone will find it and put it in his pocket. I want to make sure that Dolmain receives it."

"Send it to him," Crumm said.

"Anonymously, you mean."

"Eh? I mean in a plain wrapper with no name, milady."

"He would recognize my servants' livery."

"Thing to do," Crumm said, "I'll have one of my friends drop it on his doorstep, give the knocker a rap, and run. The household is bound to be up with such wicked goings-on."

Caro glanced at the longcase clock in the corner.

124

It was nearly midnight. Dolmain should be home from the ball by now.

"Very well, Crumm, do it at once. And make sure the brooch is wrapped in Lady Helen's handkerchief. Oh, and you had best slip out the back door, for I am being followed again. How long will it take to find one of your . . . er, friends?"

A broad grin split Crumm's face, giving him the air of a gargoyle. "Happens Ned Stork is in the kitchen now, milady. We was going to go out for a bit of a celebration after you got home. Nay, now, don't blanch and tremble so, madam. No one got a look at Ned tonight. Why, Townshend hisself could walk into that kitchen and not blink an eye. Ned ain't known as a murderer or a thief. He just lends a cove a rattler and prads upon occasion. Nothing illegal in that, eh?"

"To be sure, quite unexceptionable," she said in a choked voice. She suspected what the carriage and horses were used for, and that Ned Stork took a share of the illicit proceeds.

Crumm wrapped the brooch carefully in the handkerchief. "I will come home before we go out to celebrate, to let you know that all went well, milady. If my services are not further required, I'll leave ye now—via the back door."

"Thank you, Crumm."

He left, and the others exchanged a stricken look.

"Looks like it is going to be a long night," Newt said, reaching for the wine bottle.

In half an hour Crumm returned to announce that the plan had gone off without a hitch, as his plans always did. Ned had done exactly as he had been told. After leaving the brooch in the handkerchief on the doorstep, he had used the knocker, then darted behind the yews to see that the door was answered. When the butler came out, Dolmain was not a pace behind him. The butler had picked up the handkerchief and handed it to Dolmain. In their surprise, they had not even bothered to look into the street to see who had left it. Ned Stork had told Crumm that his lordship looked "stricken all of a heap when he opened the handkerchee and spotted the sparklers."

Caroline was so relieved, she gave Crumm twice his usual bonus. He left with his pockets jingling and a smile on his vast, misshapen face. The excitement was over for the night.

Newt said, "I will call early in the morning. I am on nettles to learn what Dolmain has to say now."

"And Lady Helen, too," Caroline added, but she still regretted that Crumm had not left the brooch in Miss Blanchard's pocket in the first place.

As she lay in bed with one lamp burning low, she smiled ruefully at Julian's portrait. He would have enjoyed this evening. It was quite in his style, except that he would have gone to spy on Miss Blanchard himself, and he would have known enough to leave the brooch where it was. Then she wondered what Lord Dolmain would say tomorrow. Would he come full of apologies, or would he wear his stiff face, thinking she had stolen the brooch and returned it out of fear? Perhaps he would not come—and that would be the worst of all. Sleep was a long time coming. Had she known what he would have to say when he did call, she would probably not have slept at all.

Chapter Fourteen

Caroline knew Dolmain usually went to the Horse Guards early in the morning, due to some crisis brewing there. With this in mind, she was in the breakfast parlor at eight-thirty the next day, feeling like a limp dishrag. Her mirror told her she looked nearly as fatigued as she felt. A light touch of rouge gave the illusion of color to her wan cheeks, but did nothing to conceal the purple shadows under her eyes.

At the expected sound of the door knocker, she tensed visibly. When Crumm appeared at the doorway, Dolmain was right behind him. He had not waited to be announced, but came pacing in with a distracted air about him. He stopped when he saw her looking so pale and vulnerable. He wanted to gather her up in his arms and carry her off to some safe place where neither of them would ever have to think of the necklace or scandal again, and instead he had the temerity to ask her to voluntarily pitch herself into the middle of his troubles.

"I have a great favor to ask you, Caro," he said. Not even a good morning. He sat beside her before she had time to offer him a chair, and further surprised her by gripping her two hands tightly in his, as if afraid she would run off on him.

"What is it, Dolmain?" she asked, suspecting this was his manner of apologizing after traducing her so vilely. Whatever the reason for his change of manner, she welcomed it. She spoke softly, and returned every pressure of his grip.

He closed his eyes a moment and frowned, as if collecting his thoughts. When he opened them again, she saw his worry, and noticed the haggard appearance of his pale face. Her heart opened to him in his trouble. He knew Helen was involved! That was it, and the knowledge was a perfect torment for him.

"Tell me everything," she said gently.

"I shall, but first let me apologize most humbly. How could I have been such a blind fool? Such appalling arrogance, thinking no child of mine could—" He came to a confused stop.

"Is it about Lady Helen?" she asked.

"She is a part of it, certainly, in it up to her eyebrows. Now, where shall I begin?" He took a deep breath, then began to tell his story in a plain manner. "Miss Blanchard was murdered last night when she took Helen's dog for a walk. She is fond of Rex and usually walks him every evening. She set out with a footman, but sent him home to get her a warmer shawl. Word of her death was sent to me at Lady Marlborough's. One of the neighbors recognized her and called Bow Street. Her body was taken to my house. Sometime after I had returned home—around midnight—there was a knock at the door. This was left on the doorstep," he said, drawing out the brooch, wrapped in the handkerchief.

Caroline did not interrupt his story. She just looked at the brooch and nodded to show him she realized it was the missing brooch.

"I have no idea who left it there," he continued, "but the handkerchief is Helen's. I believe it has something to do with Miss Blanchard's murder. Her money purse was not taken; it was not a robbery. In any case, it is clear you did not take the brooch. I want to apologize for what I have been thinking, and for what I have done, Caro. I must have been mad!" He shook his head, as if trying to rearrange the facts.

"When I talked to Helen after the loss of her brooch, I could not get out of my mind that you were with her again, as you were when her necklace disappeared. Much as it went against the pluck, I concluded you were involved in some manner. I disliked to believe it, but I could see no other explanation."

"It is all right, Dolmain. I understand."

"I had you followed again, and in an odd sort of way, I am glad I did, because it proves what I have always felt: that you are innocent. I know you returned here directly from the ball last night and did not leave your house."

"Did you ask Helen about the brooch?"

"I spent an hour trying to pry the truth out of her. She certainly knows something, but she was so frightened—nearly hysterical—that I could learn nothing. She was very fond of Miss Blanchard. The woman's death, and in such a brutal manner, was a great blow to her. In the end, I gave her a sleeping draft and sent her to bed. I accept, now, that she has in some manner become involved with criminals. Her evasiveness confirms it. I want to send her home to Elmhurst."

"I agree. It would be wise to take her home at once."

"The devil of it is, I cannot leave at this time. You know my work is confidential, and that it involves the Peninsular war. I was in touch with York at first light this morning, asking permission to leave London. He positively forbade it. Of course, I could not give him my precise reason for asking. And indeed I am most reluctant to leave just now, yet Helen's reputation must be protected at all costs. And her life," he added, with a grimace.

"What is it you want me to do, Dolmain?"

"Go with her," he said bluntly. "I know it is unconscionable of me to ask, after the way we have treated you."

She moved her hand, as if brushing this aside. "But Helen dislikes me. You could hardly choose a worse chaperon for her."

"Companion, not chaperon. Lady Milchamp has agreed to go as well, but she is getting on. It is pretty clear Helen has been pulling the wool over her eyes. I would not ask this of you if I felt there was any danger, Caro. I think you know that. All my staff will be on the *qui vive* to protect you and Helen. My hope is that you might become friends with her. Perhaps she will tell you what she has not told me."

"She will never tell me, of all people."

"She must be longing to unburden herself," he said simply. "I know there is no love lost between you two, but she is truly an innocent, trusting youngster that some very nasty people have got at somehow or other. I suspect it is her love of the French that was her undoing. Other than her charity work and that trip to the Pantheon, she has not associated with anyone I could conceivably consider undesirable. I introduced her only to the children of old and trusted friends. This undesirable involvement must have come through either Miss Blanchard or Bernard. You were right there, too. I now believe Helen hid both the necklace and the brooch, passed them on to someone, and told me they were stolen. Perhaps Miss Blanchard was killed because she had knowledge of it. I don't have all the answers, but I mean to get them. Bow Street is looking for Bernard."

"I agree Helen should be taken away at once, but is there no other aunt or relative you could send with her?"

He looked at her with sad resignation. "Of course. I had no right to ask it of you." He drew another weary sigh and sat a moment with his head

130

sunk on his palm. Caro had to force herself not to comfort him.

Then he looked up and said simply, "When this awful catastrophe struck, I could only think of coming to you."

Her heart gave a leap. In his trouble, Dolmain had turned to her, and she was letting him down. His daughter was in trouble. Perhaps Helen was not the unlovable chit she had been imagining. Anyone might behave badly if she was caught in the toils of criminals. She herself was lying to Dolmain now by omission, letting him believe she was ignorant of last night's doings regarding Miss Blanchard. But as her involvement was innocent, she felt it could keep for another time.

"I will go with her, Dolmain." she said, squeezing his fingers.

A spark of joy lit his eyes, then vanished aborning. "No, I should not have asked it. I came here on an impulse, for I knew I owed you an apology after all but accusing you of taking the jewels. There might be some danger, even at Elmhurst, although my feeling is that the gang is in London."

She did not argue, but only said, "We should leave under cover of darkness, in case your house is being watched."

"No, I have changed my mind. Cousin Isobel and her husband can accompany Helen. It would be good to have an extra man."

"Newt will be happy to come with us." She could see that Dolmain wanted to accept but held back, feeling it was an imposition, as indeed it was. But if you could not impose on your friends, on whom could you impose? "It is settled. For the remainder of the day, you should not let Helen leave the house. If she receives any messages, you should read them before giving them to her. You dare not put her at further risk."

A smile curved his lips, and his face softened in

131

admiration. "That is why I wanted you to go. You are awake on all suits, Caro. Intelligent, brave."

"Irresponsible," she reminded him.

"That was vexation speaking. You cut close to the bone to accuse my daughter. I suppose I feared, even then, that she was involved, or I would not have said such appalling things to you. It was infinitely mean of me."

"Yes, wasn't it? Shall I see you again before we leave?"

"I don't care if all hell breaks loose at the Horse Guards, I shall be home to see you off, and join you at Elmhurst as soon as possible."

"What time should I be ready to leave?"

"Soon after dark. Nineish?"

"I shall notify Newt."

He drew her hand to his lips and dropped a kiss in her palm, then curled her fingers around it, as if keeping it safe. "How can I thank you, my Caro?" he asked in a husky voice.

"You are too absurd," she said, but her voice shook with emotion at the way he was gazing at her. "I look forward to Elmhurst. One hears it is a fine estate."

He rose, still gazing at her. "All the old clichés are true, are they not? Money does not buy happiness."

She rose to accompany him to the door. "No, it does not, but as Julian used to say, it allows one to suffer in luxury."

He stiffened perceptibly, making her wonder what she had said to cause it. Julian! Why had she brought his name up at this point? She rattled on swiftly, to remove that question from his eyes. "I have a hundred things to do. I must cancel certain invitations I have accepted—or should I wait until we have reached Elmhurst, as it is a secret that we are leaving?"

132

"Will you cancel your outing with Alton?" he asked, and looked at her curiously.

"Alton? Oh, I had forgotten all about him."

"Good! You must drop him a note. For the rest, it might be best to wait. If you offend any hostesses, you can explain it after this is over. Lady Milchamp is not notifying anyone."

"Very well. I planned to attend the theater this evening, so no one will miss me."

They were at the doorway of the breakfast parlor. Dolmain took her hands and drew her aside. "I will miss you, Caro," he said, and pulled her into his arms for an embrace.

Her body responded instinctively to his. She was acutely aware of the pressure of his hands, stroking her back, gently pressing her against him more and more tightly, as if he would mold them together. But the embrace did not escalate to passion. His lips bruised hers with a ruthless ferocity for one brief moment, then he withdrew and just gazed at her.

His voice was husky as he said, "I will miss you very much. More than you know. God, I wish this were over."

She stroked his cheek. "Soon, Dolmain."

His fingers closed over hers. "Do you still miss him so much?" he asked.

She did not have to ask what he meant. "Not so much as I used to before I met you," she said.

"God bless you for that!"

Then he was gone. His step was lighter than when he had arrived. Caroline's heart was lighter, too, despite the ordeal ahead of her. She would not let him down. Together they would find out what was going on, and rescue Helen.

133

Chapter Fifteen

After Dolmain left, Caro sat on alone in a be-mused state, remembering the way he had looked at her, with a gaze more intimate than the touch of love. Had he seen the same glory in her eyes? His first wife would always hold some corner of his heart, as Julian would hers, but there was room for a new love, too. Even with Helen's problem looming over them, she was not entirely despondent.

She jotted a quick line off to Newt, asking him to come to Berkeley Square at once. Then she went upstairs and spoke to her maid about packing. She also wrote to Lord Alton, saying she was not feeling well, as that would also curtail any questions about her not being seen in town for a few days.

At ten o'clock Lady Georgiana descended from her chamber and was told the latest development in the case.

"I am sorry I will not be having a share in the migration to Elmhurst with you," she said. "It sounds exciting."

Caroline could not like to invite her without speaking to Dolmain first. At ten-thirty Lady Georgiana received a note from Lady Milchamp. She turned quite pink when she read it.

"Well now, what do you think of this?" she asked, and read aloud, "My dear Lady Georgiana: You are, of course, aware that Lady Winbourne will be visit-ing Lady Helen and myself at Elmhurst for a few days. We would be pleased if you would join us, if it is convenient for you. It would be nice to see you again, and talk over the old days. Sincerely, Lady Milchamp."

"Lovely, but I should mention, Georgie, that there might be a little more excitement than you bargain for," Caro cautioned. "When the Frenchies discover Lady Helen is not in London, they will not be long concluding where she is."

"I could do with a little excess of excitement after fifty years of ennui. I would be alone here, with you gone. You don't mind, Caro?"

"I'm delighted! I wanted to ask you myself."

Georgiana bustled off to prepare her trunk, and before long, Newton was shown into the saloon, panting from moving so quickly. "What has happened?" he demanded. "You dragged me away from my gammon and eggs. Have you had Townshend after you?"

"The Bow Street magistrate? No, of course not. We are going to Elmhurst to help look after Lady Helen. I do hope you can come, Newt. I told Dolmain you would."

"He has been here pestering you, has he?"

"Not pestering," she said, and filled him in on the visit.

Newt was thrilled with this opportunity of being with Lady Helen, away from the distractions of other gentlemen.

"I will have peace and quiet to get down to serious work on my epic," he said. "Daresay Lady Helen will give me a hand with the research since she is such a keen admirer of epics. Elmhurst is bound to have a library. I'll drop by Hatchard's before leaving and see what books I can pick up, just in case."

"Don't forget to bring your pistol," Caroline said, to remind him he had more pressing duties than poetry.

"Yes, by Jove. I'll culp a dozen wafers at Manton's Shooting Gallery this afternoon to hone my aim."

"We are to be at Dolmain's at nine tonight," she said.

"Pick you up at eight-thirty—or would you like me to come for dinner?" he asked hopefully. Newt's cook was not born to the apron, but Newt was too softhearted to turn him off.

"Yes, do."

"Good." He left, smiling.

The day dragged by, every minute seeming an hour, yet there was hardly time to attend to all the details involved in the visit. Notes flew from the Horse Guards to Curzon Street and Berkeley Square. With the increase in passengers, two carriages were now desirable. Newt's uncrested traveling carriage would provide some measure of anonymity. More notes were dispatched and replies sent back.

Lady Georgiana notified the stable not to send her mount around that morning. There were gowns to be chosen and packed. The ladies decided to take the minimum, sharing a small trunk between them. It was not likely that Lady Milchamp would be entertaining at this time, and if they were chased on the highway, a lightly burdened carriage could move more quickly. Georgie's cheeks were rosier than they had been in three decades. Crumm was given instructions for the running of the household during the ladies' absence.

By late afternoon, Caroline could think of nothing else to do but sit down and worry. They took dinner in their traveling clothes for convenience sake. Caroline could hardly swallow for anxiety over Dolmain and Helen. Most of all she worried that the same fate was planned for Helen as had befallen Miss Blanchard. Her dislike of the girl was gradually being replaced by pity. Helen was only

136

seventeen, and had been raised in the country. She would be an easy prey to unscrupulous criminals.

Helen was possibly the only person in London other than the murderer who knew what had happened to the diamond necklace. Whoever had conned it out of her might decide the best way to keep her silent and himself safe was to kill her. Caro shook away the frightening thought. Helen was safe at Curzon Street. In a few hours she would be out of London, heavily guarded and under cover of darkness. She would be safe.

At eight-thirty Newton sent for his carriage. The trunks were stowed, and the three passengers crept out into the night, peering over their shoulders at shadows. Dolmain, Lady Helen, and Lady Milchamp were waiting for them in the elegant Blue Saloon on Curzon Street. The ladies were already dressed for travel. Dolmain looked sober, Lady Milchamp distressed, and Helen looked as if she hardly realized what was going on.

Caroline had met Lady Milchamp before and knew her to be an elegant creature. Although she was no beauty, where nature had failed, art and science had come to her aid. A henna rinse did for her fading hair what the rouge pot did for her cheeks—gave it a lively touch of color. She had run a little to flesh, with full cheeks giving some illusion of youth. She welcomed the guests, then turned to talk to Georgiana.

Dolmain directed a commanding glance at his daughter. Helen apologized stiffly to Caroline, who accepted the speech more gracefully. Dolmain's nervous pacing betrayed his eagerness to see his daughter safely out of town. He called Caroline aside to outline the route he had decided on.

"I am sorry to see ladies strike out after dark, but there is no need to travel all night. You should be at Reigate around midnight. Stop at the White Hart there. I have had a footman go ahead to reserve rooms. I am sending four footmen with you, two with my own rig, and two with Newton's. It might be best if Helen travels with you and Newton in his rig, leaving Lady Milchamp and Lady Georgiana to go in my crested carriage." Caro nodded her agreement.

"The two carriages will stay together, of course," he continued. "We'll let mine go first. If anyone is watching, he will assume Helen is in my carriage. Do you have a pistol?"

"Newt has one in the carriage, and I brought my own, a small one Ju—Julian gave me to carry in my pocket."

"Good for Julian," he said, with a look that acknowledged her hesitation over naming him, and told her it was all right. "I hate to see you leave, my dear, but I really think—"

"The sooner we are off, the sooner Helen will be safe. Good-bye, Dolmain. I shall watch her to the best of my ability."

"I know it. What I do not know is how I can thank you."

She gave him a teasing smile. "I am sure you will think of something, milord."

"You may be very sure I will. I only wish we were alone—"

But they were not alone. Even as he spoke, Lady Milchamp came bustling forward. They were off, with fond farewells and a few last-minute warnings to take care.

Helen went out to the carriage on Newton's arm. Not knowing the arrangements had been made by Dolmain, Newt was as pleased as punch that she chose to drive with him. Dolmain's rig drew away first, with Newton's following closely behind it.

Newton shared a banquette with Caroline; Helen sat alone on the other side. He looked across the shadowy space and said, "I have begun research

138

on my epic, Lady Helen. Daresay your library at Elmhurst has some books on the subject."

Helen said, "I don't know. I only visit the French part of the library." Then she yawned, shielding her lips with her gloved fingers. *"Comme je suis fatiguée! I shall just curl up and try to sleep a little. Bonsoir."*

Newton unfolded a rug he kept in the carriage and placed it tenderly over her. He then turned to Caro, touching his finger to his lips to signal that she was not to speak. Helen's uncivil behavior did not endear her to Caro, but on the other hand, she wanted time to think, and had not anticipated much pleasure from three hours of stilted conversation with the girl. Caroline did not sleep, nor did Newton. She forced her thoughts from Dolmain to consider what they should do if they were stopped along the way. Both she and Newt were armed; they would just have to shoot their way free. When Newt was not gazing in a loverlike way across the shadows at the covered form on the other banquette, he was peering out the window for attackers. The trip was uneventful, however. There were few carriages on the road, and all appeared to be innocent. Shortly after midnight, they reached the White Hart in Reigate.

"My head will not be sorry to find a pillow," Newt said.

As Lady Helen immediately sat up, it was hard to believe she had been sleeping. "Are we here?" she asked.

A glance out the window showed no suspicious strangers lurking about. With four footmen and two grooms and Newton to guard them, the ladies made it safely into the inn and to their rooms. Helen was to share her chamber with her aunt; Caro and Georgie had the adjoining room, with Newton across the hall.

The party stopped a moment in the hallway outside their chambers to discuss plans for the morning.

Lady Milchamp said, "Dolmain was eager for us to start early. Is nine o'clock too early for you, Lady Georgiana?"

"I thought we would leave at first light," Caroline said. "Six-thirty or seven."

"Oh, not that early, surely!" Lady Milchamp exclaimed.

"Split the difference, leave at eight," Newton suggested.

After much discussion, it was agreed they would meet in a private parlor for breakfast at eight. They all breathed a sigh of relief as they went to their various chambers.

"Did you learn anything from Helen?" Georgie asked, as they prepared for bed.

"Not a thing. She curled up and pretended to be asleep. It is pretty clear she doesn't want to talk to me. I hope she opens up tomorrow. How did you get along with Lady Milchamp?"

"She has not changed one iota in thirty years. She thinks of nothing but balls and routs and fashions. She is au courant with all the gossip. It seems I would not have missed anything except three hours of rattling in a carriage if I had stayed home."

"And thank goodness for it," Caro replied.

"Certainly! I did not mean I wish we had been attacked."

They both slept soundly. Next door, Lady Milchamp also slept through the excitement of Helen's departure. They did not learn until morning that she was missing from her bed.

Chapter Sixteen

Lady Milchamp's first fear when she saw the empty pillow was that she had slept in. She picked up her hunter's watch from the bedside table, but her failing eyesight could not read the numbers by the faint light stealing through the curtained windows. When she lit the taper and saw the hour— seven o'clock—she knew she had not slept in, and she had a pretty good idea that Helen was not belowstairs having her breakfast.

She struggled out of bed, her annoyance quickly escalating to fear. Thank heavens Dolmain had convinced Lady Winbourne to come along on this wretched trip. That saucy hoyden would know what to do. She grabbed up her dressing gown and tapped on the door between their rooms, then went in, half expecting to see Helen with Caroline. In Lady Milchamp's view, those two ladies were cut from the same bolt. Wild and unmanageable, the pair of them. Helen acted nice as a nun in front of her papa, but there were odd twists in the girl. The dame disliked to say it of her own niece, but Helen was the slyest girl in the parish.

All she saw in the bed when she entered the chamber was one gray head wearing a muslin cap, and on the other pillow a tousle of black curls. She cleared her throat. When this brought no reaction, she gingerly shook Caroline's shoulder.

Caroline opened her eyes at once, looked in confusion at Lady Milchamp, then quickly sat up. "What is it?" she demanded.

"She is gone! Kidnapped out from under our noses!" Lady Milchamp exclaimed, and broke into loud sobs. "They have stolen her away. I might have been killed in my bed."

Caroline was out of bed and rushing into the next room while Lady Milchamp still sobbed and complained. Caro noticed at once that the door from the common corridor had not been forced, and the window was locked. Lady Helen's trunk was half-empty. It looked as if someone had rooted quickly through it. She saw a cup on the bedside table, bearing the dregs of cocoa.

"Is this cup yours, Lady Milchamp?" she asked.

"Yes, I had a few drops of laudanum to let me sleep. I never sleep in a strange place, and with all the responsibility ... Oh, whatever are we to do, Lady Winbourne? Poor little Helen has been kidnapped."

"She was not kidnapped. She slipped away on us."

Lady Milchamp stared, but she believed it. "You see what I have had to put up with!" she said, and fell to crying again.

"I must speak to the proprietor. He may have seen something. You write a note to Dolmain while I dress and go below."

She returned to her room and outlined the situation to Georgie while scrambling into her traveling suit. "I believe the chit left of her own free will," she said angrily.

"Thank goodness for that!"

"I am not so sure it is any better than being kidnapped. She is too young and foolish to realize the danger she has pitched herself into." As she spoke, she ran a brush through her hair, saying, "Wake up Newt as soon as you are dressed, Georgie. See if he heard anything in the night." Caroline hastened to

142

the door. She gave a rueful look at her companion. "Is this enough excitement for you?" she asked.

"More than enough," Georgie replied in a weak voice.

Belowstairs, the inn was already busy. Servants scuttled about with basins of hot water and trays of breakfast. The aroma of coffee was highly tempting. Caroline fought back the demons of fear that scratched at her mind. She went to the desk and said, "Lady Helen is missing from her room. Did you happen to see her leave?" She tried to keep her tone unemotional. If the clerk suspected there was blame to be placed, he might suddenly suffer an attack of forgetfulness.

"Yes, milady," he said, smiling. "She asked me to give you this when you came down for breakfast." He handed her a note.

Caroline's heart was pounding violently against her chest as she opened the page and read: "Dear Lady Winbourne: Please do not be angry with me, but I had to go. I am with friends, perfectly safe. Do not tell Papa. Sincerely, Lady Helen."

Caroline swallowed down her anxiety and said, "Foolish girl. She has gone off with friends, but she forgot to tell me which friends. Did you happen to see who it was?"

"Yes, your ladyship. When I asked her if her chaperon was not accompanying her—it seemed a trifle unusual for a young lady to be leaving with a gentleman at such an hour—Lady Helen told me the man was her uncle, Lord deVere. An older gentleman, tall, silver hair, distinguished. I am afraid that is all I can tell you, for they spoke French to each other."

Gone with a man, the worst possible news! "Lord deVere, of course. Thank you so much." The description matched the man Newt had seen at the Pantheon. "At what time did they leave?"

"It was pretty late, about two o'clock this morn-

143

ing." Two o'clock! Good God, they had been gone for over five hours!

"Did you happen to notice which way deVere's carriage headed when they left?" she asked, in a nearly normal voice.

"I am afraid not, milady." He lowered his tone to a whisper. "We had a couple of gentlemen arrive at that time—foxed. I would have turned them off, but Sir Aubrey's family have been coming to the White Hart forever. Had the deuce of a time getting them to bed."

"I see. Thank you, you have been very helpful." She found a coin in her pocket and handed it to him.

Her mind was seething with questions. Of course, Lord deVere was no uncle of Helen's. That he was speaking French and had been at the Pantheon suggested he was involved in the theft of the necklace. He might even have killed Miss Blanchard—and now he had Helen.

She ran upstairs to find the rest of her party assembled in Lady Milchamp's room. Three anxious faces turned to her with hopeful eagerness. It was clear they all looked to her to guide them. She already knew Lady Milchamp for a peagoose; Georgie had little experience of life. Newt would be some help, but it would be for her to direct him. From some deep well of fortitude, she must find the resources to handle the situation until Dolmain could come. He would leave the Horse Guards now, whether York gave permission or not. Necessity compelled her to damp down her own fear and confusion and take the reins.

"It is as I suspected. She left of her own accord," she said with a calmness she was far from feeling. She gave the details she had learned from the clerk. "This Lord deVere would not be an uncle on her mama's side, Lady Milchamp?"

"No, Marie was an only child."

144

"I see. Have you written to Dolmain?"

The lady handed her a note. "May I?" Caro asked, and glanced quickly through it. Lady Milchamp had written that dear little Helen had been stolen from her bed by the Frenchies, and was probably dead in a ditch by now. "Perhaps I should write a different note, now that we have learned a little more," Caro said, and threw Lady Milchamp's note into the grate.

"What can I do?" Newt asked.

"DeVere must have had a carriage. You could drive around—toward London is our best bet—and question the toll gate keepers. The clerk says there is a Sir Aubrey someone or other who arrived here at the inn as Helen was leaving. Find out his room and talk to him. He may remember something."

"What can we do?" Lady Milchamp asked.

"Try to stay calm. Have some breakfast," Caroline said.

Lady Milchamp was happy to dump the matter in Caro's dish.

"I shall order a private parlor. Come down as soon as you are dressed," Caroline said, and left with Newton.

In the parlor, Caroline wrote to Dolmain, and Newton went off to rouse Sir Aubrey and his friend while waiting for the coffee to arrive. When he returned, the coffee had come and Caroline had finished her note.

"Did you learn anything?" she asked eagerly.

"I couldn't rouse Sir Aubrey, but t'other fellow—his name is Giles something—saw Lady Helen leave right enough, and not in a carriage. There were two mounts waiting outside. He says they were good tits. Bays, he thinks."

"If they were riding, they have gotten even farther away from us! And they can avoid the toll stations by running across country. I hate to write this news, but I must tell Dolmain."

145

"Giles heard the word 'Brighton.' Speaks a bit of French. He thinks Helen asked how long it would take to get to Brighton."

"Brighton? That is excellent! It is much smaller than London. Looking for her in London would be like looking for a needle in a haystack."

"No, a diamond in a haystack," Newt said, and sighed.

While Caroline added the necessary items to her note, Newt sat, his protuberant eyes diminished to slits and his face clenched in wrinkles. When she put down her pen, he spoke.

"Thing to do, go to Brighton," he said.

"I have asked Dolmain to meet us at the Royal Crescent on Marine Parade. We'll be there by noon if we leave soon."

"If we can get a burr under the old girls' saddles."

"We cannot wait for them, Newt. We shall leave at once, and let them follow or go back to London if they prefer. I should have insisted on sharing Helen's room. Lady Milchamp is useless. She quacked herself with laudanum, imagine!"

Caroline ran upstairs to speak to Georgiana, who stood waiting while Lady Milchamp fiddled with her coiffure.

"So difficult, coming without a dresser," the dame complained. "Oh, there you are, Lady Winbourne," she said in a plaintive voice. "Have you found Helen?"

The inanity of the question was enough to show the nature of the lady's mind. Caroline outlined briefly what Newton had learned, and what she intended to do.

"What, leave without breakfast?" Lady Milchamp exclaimed.

"You and Lady Georgiana eat here and follow us at your leisure later, or return to London if you like."

"We will follow you," Georgie said, before Lady

Milchamp could choose the less exciting course. "I will pack your trunk for you, Caro. You and Newt will not want to waste a minute."

"Why go to a hotel?" was Lady Milchamp's next objection. "Dolmain has a house on the Marine Parade."

"I did not know where his house was situated. Why do you not go there, ma'am? We can join you there later," Caro said.

"That will be best," Georgie said. She could see Caro was on thorns to be off. "Run along, dear. Godspeed."

Caro gave her a quick hug and ran off.

Lady Milchamp said crossly, "I thought we might count on Lady Winbourne to prevent this sort of thing. This will do Helen's reputation no good. I had hoped to nab the Duke of Clive for her. Forty thousand a year and three estates. Dolmain must not blame me if the girl has disgraced herself."

Newton had his carriage waiting when Caroline joined him. "We are one footman short as you sent one to London with your note," he said. "I am taking two with me. The old girls can make do with one, eh? Not likely anyone will molest them."

"If I had known Lady Milchamp was a fool, I would have asked Dolmain to leave her at home."

"I have had a thermos of coffee put in the carriage. You'd best have a cup. Your nerves are in tatters, Caro."

They entered the carriage and Ankel sprang the horses.

"Try if you can rest now," Caro said.

"Couldn't sleep if my life depended on it. And neither could you." He felt tears stinging his eyes, as if he had been eating green gooseberries, to think of poor little Helen at the mercy of DeVere.

"No, I couldn't," she said, and poured a cup of coffee.

Chapter Seventeen

Even with a team of four good nags, the trip took four hours. Four hours was a long time to be rattled about in a confined space, worrying. Once through Tilgate Forest, they stopped from time to time to inquire at the toll gates, but heard nothing of their quarry. Their spirits were low and their stomachs hollow by the time they reached Hayward's Heath, a little past the midway point of their trip.

"My stomach has begun asking my throat if it's been cut," Newt said. "Time for fork work, Caro. If I don't sink a bicuspid into a beefsteak, I will be no good to man or beast."

"Yes," she agreed. She needed a respite from the jostling of a carriage going full tilt, and perhaps a cup of tea.

The hamlet boasted no major hostelry. They stopped at a small inn. The servant was a bright-eyed young girl who looked as if not much would escape her.

"I don't suppose a young lady and her uncle stopped here last night around three o'clock?" Caroline asked.

To her astonishment, the girl said, "Indeed they did. I didn't serve them myself; Meg told me about them. The lady was ever so pretty. The gentleman tipped Meg a golden boy."

"A blond lady, wearing a green traveling suit?"

Caro asked, naming the outfit missing from Helen's trunk.

"That's her."

Having finally received confirmation of her theory, Caro hardly knew what else to ask.

"Friends of ours," Newton said. "Set out on horseback. Still riding, were they? Or did they switch to a carriage?"

"They changed nags, but went on their way on horseback," the servant replied.

"Hired the nags here, did they?" Newt asked.

"Oh no, sir. We have nothing good enough for the likes of Lord deVere. He brought four mounts here in the afternoon. He rode off on one late last night, leading t'other behind him, then come back with the young lady riding it. They had a bite and a drink, and left straightaway on the fresh mounts. Early this morning his lordship's groom took away the ones him and his niece had been riding last night.

"I expect Lord deVere and his niece were in a hurry to get to Brighton?" Caroline asked, adopting a conversational tone.

"They never spoke a word of English, according to Meg. Meg did hear the young lady say something about her mama and papa. She figured the lady was going home, wherever home might be for a French lady nowadays. She seemed eager to be getting on."

"Yes, very eager," Caroline said in a thin voice. She thanked the servant, who then left.

"Crafty devil," Newt grumbled. "If he'd hired a rig or even nags, we might have found out where he was going. The stable would have wanted an address."

"That is precisely why he brought his own. We are not dealing with an amateur, Newt. This was all planned in advance. Helen got a note to her cohorts before we left London, letting them know we would be stopping at Reigate."

"The thing took time to set up. She must have used a servant she trusts to send her message."

"I wish I had known this. Dolmain might have questioned his staff and discovered something. I shall tell him as soon as we meet in Brighton. Are you finished breakfast?"

"I can take the rest with me," he said, and wrapped a piece of plum cake up in a napkin. In her distraction, Caroline had not noticed what he was eating. "Just to keep up my strength," he explained, when she eyed it askance. "The servant said a beefsteak would take fifteen minutes to cook."

"At least we know we are on the right track," he said, when they were back in the flying carriage. "Pity we don't have an address. Plenty of places to hide, even in Brighton."

"Dolmain might have some ideas."

But when Dolmain finally arrived at the Royal Crescent at one o'clock, he was in such a state, he hardly knew his name, much less where his daughter could be. He had driven his sporting carriage, which made better time than a traveling coach. Caroline felt a heavy ache in her heart to see him so anxious. His face was chalk white with the strain and worry. His expression did not improve when she outlined what she had learned, including that DeVere was the same man who had been at the Pantheon with Helen. Caro felt in some manner it was her fault, but when she apologized, he brushed her words aside.

"This is my fault. You tried to tell me, but I refused to believe my daughter was capable of subterfuge. I had no right to ask you to put yourself in jeopardy for her sake. It is I who must apologize, Caro. I have not spent enough time with her. She has turned to these people in her loneliness."

"Don't blame yourself. How should Helen be lonely, when she had the excitement of her debut? She could have been busy every minute if she had wanted to." Caro wanted to ease his suffering, but this was not the time for false comfort. There was a job to do, so she damped down her compassion and said sternly, "Have you eaten yet today?"

"I don't know. Some coffee, I think . . ." he said vaguely.

"We've not had a bite ourselves, barring a piece of plum cake," Newt said. "We have ordered up a beefsteak."

"And you shall have some of it, too, while I tell you what we know," Caroline said. "I fear it is not much," she added swiftly, when his eyes flew hopefully to hers.

While waiting for lunch, she briefly outlined the recent events over a glass of wine. Dolmain listened closely.

"Then it is clear she went of her own accord, and that she is somewhere in Brighton. I shall interrogate the servants in London about that message Helen smuggled out of the house, or perhaps write my butler asking him to do it. I wish I could be there myself. You have done an admirable job, Caro."

Her heart swelled at his praise. "Thank you, but the job is not done yet. Have you any idea where she could be in Brighton? Does Helen have special friends she might go to?"

"Our friends are in London, with the Season beginning. In Brighton we stay at my house. We must look there, but I cannot believe she would take this man to my home."

"She might. She doesn't know we know she has come to Brighton. Let us go," Caro said, jumping up from the table.

"I shall go," he said, gently pushing her back onto her chair. "You shall have your breakfast."

151

She did not urge him to stay and eat. Of course he must continue looking for his daughter. She had no appetite herself, but nibbled at her peas and potatoes, which seemed to go down more easily than meat. Newt ate stolidly without speaking, which left her free to think. Helen had mentioned Brighton the day they went shopping. Her mama and papa met here. Dolmain had bought the house his wife had been living in for her, and later given it to the French émigrés. But what was the address? Dolmain was back before they left the table.

"She is not there," he said. "I keep the place open from April until October. The Lorimers will send word here if she comes. I cannot think it likely."

"Nor can I," Caro said. "But the house where your wife used to live here in Brighton, do you remember the address?"

His face closed up like a fist. "Bartholomew Avenue. The place was sold years ago. How do you come to know of it?"

"Helen said you gave it to the French. They still use it."

"She is mistaken."

"But surely it is worth a look!"

"There is something you must know about Helen," he said grimly. "She lives in a dreamworld of her own devising. She imagines her mama and I lived some idyll of true love. That was far from being the case. When her mother . . . left us, I saw no need to tell Helen the savage truth at such a young age. Marie ran off with a Frenchman when we were in Paris. I had been sent there on a job for the government. Her leaving was no surprise, to tell the truth."

"I am sorry," Caro said.

He brushed it aside. "Marie and I soon learned we did not suit. Our marriage was a hell. I was a young fool, marrying a lady I scarcely knew. I told Helen her mother had to return to France for patriotic reasons. When Marie died, I told my daughter I had word of her death in France, thinking that would be the end of it. Instead, she turned her mother into a martyr, a sort of cross between Saint Joan and Venus. Marie was pretty. Helen even set up a shrine to her. I did not give the house to the French. It was sold to a boot-maker. I had hoped that a strict upbringing would prevent Helen from developing certain traits she might have inherited from her mother. If I was determined to see no fault in her, that was the cause."

"I see." Caro sat, stunned. Why had Helen told her such a plumper? Was she afraid Dolmain meant to saddle her with a stepmama? She must realize he had to marry to ensure an heir.

Dolmain seemed eager to quit the subject. "What was it the servant at Hayward's Heath said about Helen mentioning me?"

"She said something about her mama and papa. As Helen was speaking French, Meg only caught the odd word."

"It seems clear the notion behind this is to extract money from me for her safe return. The kidnapper—I will call him that, for perverting a child's mind is another way of stealing her from her parent—the kidnapper will write to me in London demanding payment. I should not have come here."

"This is where deVere was bringing Helen."

"There isn't time to ransack every house and barn and stable until we find her. The note will go to my London house. He has colleagues there. I must return to London at once. I shall interrogate the servants about that message Helen sent and speak to my banker about assembling the money as well."

Caro had to bite her lip to keep from speaking. He was too fagged for another trip. He should rest and eat something.

"Yes, you must go, of course. Newt and I shall stay here and try to discover where she is."

"Don't take any more chances," he said.

He rose immediately. She accompanied him to the door to have a moment alone with him. "Your aunt and Georgie are going to Marine Parade," she said. "Shall I join them there?"

He rubbed his brow. "Of course. I should have asked you to. My mind is so full of this ... torment." He seized her two hands and squeezed them tightly. "I do not believe Helen is the conniving creature this stunt suggests. Someone is exploiting her idolization of Marie. As I think over the past, I realize it was shortly after Miss Blanchard came to us that Helen set up that shrine in her bechamber. I wonder whether Miss Blanchard was not preying on her weakness, encouraging her in this folly. I should have told Helen the truth. I wanted to protect her from the sordid facts."

"One worry at a time, Dolmain. Find her, then give both Helen and yourself a good scold for past indiscretions."

"I shall go, but first you must promise me you will not do anything dangerous. *Promise* me, Caro. I could not bear it if anything happened to you."

The naked fear in his eyes struck her deeply. "I promise," she said. But it was not a promise she felt obliged to keep. His expression constituted emotional coercion. "Now, go."

He did not reply or say good-bye, but just gazed at her a moment, as if storing up this image of sanity, then he turned and strode quickly out of the hotel.

After breakfast, Newt decided to scour Brighton, looking for Helen. Caroline opted to go to Dolmain's house. She did not think deVere would let Helen roam the streets. He would keep her confined by either force or trickery.

Lady Milchamp and Georgiana had arrived and

were having tea when Caroline reached Marine Parade. Dolmain's house was a handsome mansion, less formal than Dolmain House in London. Some ancestor, perhaps influenced by the Prince Regent's pavilion, had done the saloon up in lacquered furnishings and other tokens of chinoiserie. Lady Milchamp looked up from her teacup and asked, "Have you found her, Lady Winbourne?"

"No, ma'am, but I have spoken to Dolmain." She explained that he had returned to London in expectation of receiving a ransom note, and to question the servants.

"I knew from the first time I laid eyes on her that Marie-Hélène would be the ruination of Dolmain one way or the other," Lady Milchamp declared. "She was monstrously pretty, of course, but five years older than Dolmain, and sly. That is how Helen comes by her deceitful nature. I never thought Marie would so forget herself as to run off with a penniless fellow. Mind you, she took plenty of jewelry with her."

Caroline was interested to learn what she could of Lady Dolmain—strange no one ever called her that. It was as if the family wanted to deny the relationship. She understood now why Dolmain seldom spoke of his wife. It was not sorrow at a love lost, but regret and shame of his own folly. Perhaps that was why he was reluctant to marry again, especially for love.

"How did she die, Lady Milchamp?" she asked.

"She drowned at Weymouth. She and her fellow ran off to Paris, but when the money ran out, she returned to London and tried to patch things up with Dolmain. Of course, he would not have her back. She did not ask for a divorce, and he was not eager for one because of the damage the scandal would do to Helen's chances. He paid her a handsome allowance to keep out of London and away from Elmhurst. She settled in Weymouth with her fancy man, calling herself Madame Bellefeuille, her so-called husband's name. They got caught in a storm during a yachting party. Bellefeuille made it to shore, but Marie could not swim. The solicitor who was handling matters notified Dolmain of her death as Bellefeuille could not afford the funeral. Bellefeuille had the gall to ask Dolmain to continue the allowance. Can you beat that for brass? He threatened to tell the world the whole story. Dolmain told him to go to the devil. Marie is buried in Weymouth."

"He never told Helen any of this?" Caroline asked.

"No, my dear. He told her he had had word from France of Marie's death. Only the family knows the truth. We let it out that Marie had died. People were too kind to ask for details, and of course, interest in her had dwindled by then. It was five years ago that she died. A blessing really, for of course, Dolmain must make another match to provide an heir. He thought Lady Mary Swann might do, but that did not come off."

"Could Bellefeuille be the man behind this scheme?" Caroline asked.

"I shouldn't be the least surprised. He pestered Dolmain for money for a year or so. Dolmain held fast. He can be stubborn as a mule when he gets his back up. I have no idea what happened to Bellefeuille."

"What did he look like?"

"I heard he was a handsome rascal. Marie was susceptible to a handsome face. He was tall, distinguished-looking."

"What age would he be now?"

"In his forties. Why do you ask, Lady Winbourne?"

"Lord deVere is a tall, distinguished-looking gentleman with silver at his temples."

"It could be him!" Lady Milchamp exclaimed.

"That would explain why Helen was chosen for this wretched scheme. She is only a means of screwing money out of Dolmain. We must tell him your idea, Lady Winbourne."

"It is not much help, but at least Dolmain knows what Bellefeuille looks like, and might know his habits. Where he might have Helen hidden, I mean. I shall notify him."

"Do that, dear. I must lie down, for I am rattled to pieces. You look burned to the socket as well, Lady Georgiana."

Lady Milchamp left and Caro wrote the note to Dolmain.

"Is there anything I can do?" Georgie asked, when she had dispatched the note.

"Waiting is the ladies' job, and no easy one. Oh, here is Newt!" she exclaimed, as he came pouncing in, big with news. Both ladies looked at him expectantly. "What is it?" Caro demanded. "Have you found her?"

"No, but I have got a lead!"

Chapter Eighteen

"What is it?" Caroline exclaimed.

"You remember the lady who was talking to Helen and Blanchard at the Pantheon. The good-looking one, Renée?"

"Yes, have you seen her? Was she with deVere?"

"What would deVere be doing in a millinery shop? She was alone. Bought a bonnet, peacock blue, with a dangling feather."

"I hope you followed her when she came out."

"I did, and you'll never guess where she went."

"To the cottage on Bartholomew Avenue," Caroline said. It was the only address in Brighton Helen had ever mentioned.

"If you already knew where they have her, why have we been wasting all this time?"

"It was an educated guess."

Georgiana cleared her throat and said, "Did Dolmain not tell you that cottage had been sold to a boot-maker, Caro?"

"Yes, but Helen said there were French émigrés living in it. Perhaps it has been sold again, or rented. I wager Bellefeuille was the Frenchie she was referring to."

"Bellefeuille?" Newt asked. "You mean Lord deVere."

Caro told him what she had learned from Lady Milchamp, and her idea that deVere was Monsieur Bellefeuille, trying a new trick to get money from Dolmain.

"Thing to do," Newt said, "send in a constable."

Georgie said, "I am not versed in law, but I do not believe the fellow could be charged with kidnapping when Helen went voluntarily. You might find her, but as Dolmain is not here to force her to return, it might only result in her darting off with Bellefeuille again. Do not count on her to help you get him arrested. She will swear he is her uncle, or some such thing. He might even induce her to marry him, giving him complete control of her and her fortune. She might be harmed physically," she added discreetly.

Newt's face faded from pink to white as the dame spoke. "If the bleater harms a hair on her head, I shall shoot him."

"And end up on the gibbet," Georgie said calmly.

"We do not know for certain that Helen is there," Caro said. "If they have her secreted somewhere else, we have only alerted them that we are on to them, and given them time to make other plans, or get away."

"For that matter," Georgie said, "we do not actually know that the lady in the peacock bonnet is involved. There was no lady with deVere when he took Helen away from Reigate. I would not like to tip my hand until more is learned."

"You certainly know how to take the wind out of a fellow's sails," Newt said. "I am off to keep a watch on the house."

"No!" Caroline said, in the authoritative voice that told them she had resumed command of the operation. "They will spot you, Newt. You must wear a disguise. A fishmonger—the streets here in Brighton are full of them. In that way, you could actually go to the back door and ask if they wanted to buy some fish. You might learn something from the servants."

"Where would I get the fish?"

"At the fish market," Caroline replied. "Buy enough to fill a basket and set up as a fishmonger."

"They talk funny," Newt said, frowning deeply.

Caroline felt the blood singing through her veins. Why should she not be a fishmonger? Plenty of fishermen passed the job of selling along to their daughters, and without undue pride, she felt she could do a better job of acting than Newt.

"Someone ought to be there now," Georgie said.

Newt was fidgeting about impatiently. "She is right," he said. "The important thing is to see they don't spirit Helen off. Dash it, we know she came to Brighton. She mentioned that very house. That is where the bounders have her."

"Yes, you are right," Caro agreed. "It will take time to don a disguise and buy the fish. You guard the house, Newt, and I shall pose as a fishmonger. Stay outside to make sure I come out alive," she added unthinkingly.

"Now, Caro!" Georgie exclaimed. "It is all well and good to help Helen, but to be throwing yourself at kidnappers and worse—deVere might take advantage of you."

"He will not be attracted to a street urchin reeking of fish," Caro said. "Now, where shall I begin? I must ask Lorimer to buy a basket of fish. I can beg or borrow a servants' gown and roll it in the dust. A mobcap to cover my hair."

"I am off," Newt said. "I mean to camp out in the Town Hall. One of the windows on the north side will give me a view of the house. If deVere leaves with Helen, I will be on him like a burr on a dog's tail."

When he had left, Caro said to Georgie, "Would you mind writing to Dolmain to tell him what Newt has learned, and what we are— No, don't tell him what we are doing. He will only worry. Just tell him that we believe deVere is Bellefeuille, and that the lady we saw at the Pantheon is here in Brighton."

"Very well. I shall send the note off at once."

Caroline went down to the kitchen to speak to Mrs. Lorimer. "Would you please have Lorimer run over to the fish market to buy a large basket of fish, and do you have an old gown I could buy or borrow?" she asked. "The older, the better. And I shall need a mobcab as well. It is extremely urgent."

Mrs. Lorimer, an old and trusted family servant, knew of the crisis afoot and was informed of Caroline's plan. "Anything, if it will help to find little Helen," she said, and called for Lorimer to go fetch a basket of fish.

She had a mobcap and sacrificed a gray muslin gown she had been saving to make into dustrags. Caro took them into the yard and gave them a thrashing in the dust. Mrs. Lorimer watched in consternation as Lady Winbourne gathered up a bowl of dust and shook it over her lovely raven hair until it lost its sheen, then applied it to her face as if it were powder. When Caro undertook a job, she did it wholeheartedly. She knew the only hope of pulling this rig off was to forget she was Lady Winbourne and become a seller of fish. As she worked, her ladylike expression changed to a pert, insouciant grin.

"How's that then, mum?" she asked, peeking at Mrs. Lorimer when she had finished the transformation.

"I would never recognize you, milady. Wherever did you learn to speak like that?"

Caro's impish grin softened to nostalgia. "My husband and I were footmen to Lord and Lady Carlisle for a whole weekend," she said, remembering a bet Julian had made with a friend that he and Caro would never spend another night under Lord Carlisle's roof after defeating the man's bill in Par-

161

liament. They had masqueraded as servants and spent the hardest weekend of their lives fetching and carrying. But Julian had won the bet, and she had learned to speak like a servant.

"Some joke, I wager," Mrs. Lorimer said. "But your hands, milady," she said, looking at Caroline's dainty white hands with the manicured fingernails. "Wear an old pair of gloves. My gardening gloves are in wretched shape, with the thumb out."

"Excellent!"

"And your teeth—a girl of the lower orders would not have teeth in such good repair."

"I refuse to have a tooth drawn! I shan't smile. You must tell me what price fish fetches hereabouts. I want to offer a bargain, to entice the cook to let me into the kitchen."

It was half an hour later that a fishmonger dressed in a form-concealing gray dress left the back door of Dolmain's house on Marine Parade with her basket of fish holding turbot, mullet, winkles, and mussels hung over her neck, and scampered westward to Bartholomew Avenue. No one gave her more than a passing glance. When Newton, watching from a north window of the Town Hall, saw a fishmonger enter the watched cottage, he peered closely at her. It was not until the mobcab turned and stared up at the window that he was certain it was Caro. By Jove, she should be on the stage. How naturally she swung her little rump, like a regular hoyden. He checked his watch when she went down the lane to the back door. If she was not out in fifteen minutes or so, he would go after her.

Caro was surprised to see the little flint cottage was in such poor repair. The roof sagged, the paint was chipped, and the garden all overgrown. When the back door opened, she was taken aback to find not a cook or housekeeper staring at her, but a woman who matched Newt's description of Renée.

She was pretty, but of a certain age, and wearing a good deal of paint on her face. Her gown, featuring an excess of bows and lace, was too smartly vulgar for real fashion. A tea towel tucked in around her waist was her only concession to the kitchen.

"Fresh fish, mum?" Caro asked, taking care not to reveal her teeth. "Come in my pa's boat this mornin'. Lovely bit of turbot, that," she said, holding the rounded, flat-bodied fish up by the gills. She was glad she was wearing gloves. The fish were slimy.

The woman looked at it with distaste. "Disgusting! But then, one must eat something, *hein?* How does one prepare it?" she asked, revealing a trace of French accent.

"Oh, poached, mum, with white sauce. A crying shame to bake a turbot. I could let you have this beauty for eight shillings. A rare price for a middling-sized fish. They're the tenderest. You could feed eight people off'n this lad."

"It is too large. I only have to feed three." Caroline schooled her features to indifference, lowering her head lest her eyes betray her interest. Three! Herself, deVere, and Helen.

"Serve it up with a cream sauce tomorrow, then," she suggested. "It'll keep overnight in the larder."

"I don't plan to be here tomorrow." Again Caro had to school her face to vacuity.

"Pity. How about some nice mussels then, mum?"

The woman studied the turbot. It would save a trip out to shop for food. There were potatoes in the larder. "Just poach it, you say?"

"Yes, mum." With some memory of her childhood days in cook's kitchen, she added, "You wash it in salt water first to get rid of the slime, and then rub it in lemon before you boil it."

"How long do you boil it?"

"For this one, half an hour," Caro said at random. "I dislike to touch it, yet if it only has to be

163

poached . . ." She disliked to contemplate dealing with an oven.

"Your cook run off on you, did she?" Caro asked pertly.

"Exactly. I don't suppose you—"

Caro's heart leapt at this unexpected piece of luck. The woman wanted her to prepare the fish— but how could she do it without removing her gloves? She felt a note of reluctance was called for and said, "I've got my living to earn, mum."

"I shall pay you. Wash the thing off with salt and put it in the pot. I shan't be able to eat a bite, I know. Much he cares for me, so long as *she* likes it. How much altogether?"

"A guinea."

"A pound. Prepare the fish and sauce and leave them on the table. I shall pay you after you have finished."

It was too good an opportunity to lose. "Very well."

The woman removed the tea towel from her waist and walked quickly from the room. Afraid that she might return to check on her progress, Caroline used a tea towel to rub the fish down with salt and rinsed it off. Finding no lemon, she put the turbot on the rack in a poaching pot and added water. White sauce was a mystery to her. Before attempting it, she ran halfway up the back stairs to see what she could learn.

"She is sleeping?" the woman asked in French.

A man's voice replied, also in French. "I put laudanum in her tea. That should hold her until dinner at nine."

"How long will it take him to collect the money?"

"We should have it by midnight. Which means another of your wretched dinners, Renée."

"I don't see why you and I cannot go out to dine."

"And leave our little gold mine all alone? No, we shall all dine here tonight, feeding her plenty of

164

wine, then send her back upstairs to rest. We have to keep her convinced we are her true friends. I doubt her own papa could lure her away, after the job I have done convincing her."

"It seems cruel to get her hopes up." Caroline's ears perked up at this. What ruse had they used to convince Helen to go with them?

"I owe milord a lesson," deVere/Bellefeuille said in a sneering voice. "And it will cost him more than pounds and pence this time." Caro felt the hair on the back of her neck rise at that frightening speech.

Instead of following up this line, Renée said, "I must prepare the sauce for the turbot."

Caroline scampered back down to the kitchen. White sauce! Presumably it was made from milk or cream. She remembered seeing cook make blancmange with cornstarch. When the woman returned to the kitchen, Caro was filling a pan with milk.

"Your fish is ready to go," she said. "I'm just getting on with the sauce."

The woman watched as she rattled about the cupboards. She found a tin of cornstarch and plunged her hands into it to conceal their natural whiteness. She used half of the powder to make a paste, which she added to thicken the milk. The brew soon thickened to an alarming degree over the stove.

The woman came to look at it. "It's time to thin it now," Caro said, and added water until it was of more or less the proper consistency.

"You've only to set it aside and heat it up at dinnertime," she said, with a sigh of relief. Now she could leave.

She was about to go when she heard a voice from the bottom of the stairs. "So this is how *you* are preparing the sauce, Renée," deVere said. She hadn't heard his approach.

They both spoke French as before. Renée replied, "I never claimed to be a cook, *mon chéri.*"

"Soon we shall have all the servants your greedy little heart desires—if you have a heart, *c'est à dire.*"

Caro turned her back to them, pulled on her gloves, and picked up her basket.

"You pay her, Michel," the woman said. "A pound."

DeVere rattled some coins in his pocket, drew out his hand, and came toward Caro. Her heart floated up to her throat. He could not recognize her! He had never seen her. Oh, but if he recognized she was a lady . . .

"You're a pretty little thing," he said, pulling her chin up between his fingers. She twitched her head away. "A temper, eh? I like that in a girl." His sharp eyes traveled in a leisurely way down to her bosoms. "Or should I say, woman? With a bath and a decent gown . . ."

"Let her go, lecher," Renée said angrily.

DeVere dropped the coin in her gloved fingers. "Thankee, sir," she said, swallowing a prayer of thanks for Madame's jealousy. She hung the fish basket around her neck and fled out the back door. As she left, she heard Renée light into him for his lechery. "You never can keep your vile hands off a woman!"

Without waiting to hear his reply, Caro darted down the lane and back onto the street just as Newton came around the corner. She scuttled along the street and they both turned the corner beyond view of the house on Bartholomew Avenue.

"Is that you, underneath all the dirt?" Newt asked, peering owlishly at her.

"Of course it is! Helen is there!" she exclaimed.

"Let us go fetch her."

"She is drugged, but I have a plan."

"Good, dump that load of fish and let us hear it."

"We can safely leave her for the moment. Let us

166

go to Marine Parade. I want a long bath to kill the stench."

"Damme, I don't want an open basket of fish in my carriage."

"I shall leave it on the street. It won't remain there long." She removed the basket and put it in the shade. A young tousle-haired boy looked at it hopefully. "Take it," she said.

"For free?"

"No, for a pound." She handed him the coin deVere had given her. She didn't want to keep anything he had touched.

"Gorblimey," the urchin said, and snapping up the coin and fish basket, he lit out down the street at a gallop.

Chapter Nineteen

"We shall need a ladder and a blond wig and some stout ropes," Caroline said, as they drove to Marine Parade. "It would help if we had a portrait of her. I wonder if Helen has not got a copy of one at Marine Parade."

"The stench of fish has disordered your brain, my girl," Newt said severely. "Here, let me get some air into the rig." So saying, he opened both windows.

"If there is no picture, then Lady Milchamp must give me a description of her," Caro continued, thinking out loud.

"Deuce take it, Caro, you know what Helen looks like. And if you are thinking of wearing a wig and breaking into the house on Bartholomew Avenue—"

"Not breaking in!" she said. "I promised Dolmain I would not do anything rash. I am merely planning to lure Helen out."

"You figure she is that fond of ropes and ladders?"

"No, goose. The ladder is to reach her window, and the rope is in case we have to force her to come with us."

"A good thing you ain't planning anything dangerous!" he said, with heavy irony.

"It is not in the least dangerous. I plan to dress up like her mama. I am convinced that is the lady Helen thinks she will be meeting in Brighton. Meg heard her mention her mama and papa. She adores her mama. Dolmain told her her mother died in

France. How easy for deVere to pretend he has found her and brought her back alive. It must have been Miss Blanchard who told him of Helen's devotion to her mother. In fact, it was after Blanchard came to them that Helen set up the shrine. I daresay Blanchard encouraged her."

"Silly thing to do. The woman ain't a saint. But why did Helen not tell Dolmain they had found his wife?"

"Because if Helen had told her papa that Marie had turned up, Dolmain would reveal it for a lie. DeVere has given Helen some excuse for not telling Dolmain, and convinced her to steal a valuable necklace to secure her mama's safety."

"Just what is it again that the wig has to do with it?"

"I am going to rig myself up to look like Lady Dolmain to fool Helen. In the dark, just a glimpse through a window. As Helen will be in her bedchamber, we shall require a ladder to reach it. If I could copy the hairdo and gown Marie is wearing in the portrait, it would work. Helen can have no real memory of her mama. What she remembers is a portrait. I wish I had seen it. If she saw a similar-looking woman, she would at least open the window, and if we cannot convince her to come with us, we shall just have to snatch her and steal her away."

Newt considered this. "Might work," he allowed, "but we will need some excuse for going to the window instead of to the door. The mama is supposed to be friendly with deVere. No need for her to go scrambling up ladders to see her daughter."

"Surely we can invent a convincing lie as well as he! They plan to feed Helen a good deal of wine. She will be groggy, which is all to the good. I shall say some spies are lurking outside the door to kill Lady Dolmain when she arrives, and that deVere wants them—us—to leave by the window."

"As I said, might work; on t'other hand, she might recognize you and holler, bringing deVere down on our heads. Or deVere might hear us going up the ladder, or—well, any number of things, every one of them dangerous for you."

"Or they might fool Dolmain into handing over the ransom money and not give Helen back at all," she shot back. "DeVere said this affair would cost Dolmain more than pounds and pence. You should have heard the way he said it, Newt, so gloating. God only knows what he meant, but I fear it does not bode well for Helen. We must save her, and Georgie has made clear there is no point calling in Bow Street. I know Dolmain will fly both ways, but I do not see how he can be here much before midnight.

"It might be best to let him handle it, though. His daughter, after all. If anything goes wrong . . ."

"He was in such a state when he left. I fear he will do something rash and get himself killed. I would like to have it all over before he gets here."

"I hope it ain't all over for you, my girl. Biting off more than you can chew, but between the two of us, we might manage to chew it up and spit it out. You can count on me. Anything for Helen." He lifted his fat chin and added nobly, "King Arthur, I daresay, would do no less."

She tweaked his ear. "What an excellent cousin you are. I shall buy you a round table if we succeed." And I shall talk Dolmain down out of the boughs for countermanding his orders, she added to herself.

When they reached Marine Parade, the first item of business was to assure Lady Milchamp that Helen was alive, but in danger. The second was to outline the plan, and discover whether there was a likeness of Lady Dolmain in the house.

"In Lady Helen's room," Lady Milchamp said. "A smaller copy taken from the original. Helen had it done so that she would always have a picture of her mama. It is not so good as the Lawrence portrait, of course, but quite like."

"May I see it, ma'am?" Caro asked.

Mrs. Lorimer was sent to fetch it. Caroline was accustomed to hearing herself called beautiful, but the lady in the portrait took her breath away. Her hair was a cloud of golden curls encircling a heart-shaped face. A band of laurel leaves sat on her head like a crown. Long-lashed emerald green eyes gazed serenely out at the world. The full lips were drawn up in a small, seductive smile.

"No wonder Dolmain fell in love with her," Caroline said.

"The original flattered her; this copy gilds the lily. Her eyes were not that large and much lighter, though it is true the whole city was running mad for her," Lady Milchamp said, which did little to restore Caro's confidence.

But she had a job to do, and settled down to study the portrait with a view to imitating the hairstyle and gown. There was, alas, no hope of her face suddenly turning into a heart shape, or her eyes doubling in size. The hair was the most distinguishing feature, however, and it was capable of being copied in a wig. The gown would be even easier to duplicate. A simple band of white rolled gauze encircled her shoulders and nestled between an enviable pair of breasts, like two satin melons. A few inches of green material had been sketched in below the white collar. She wore no jewelry save a pair of pearl drops at her ears.

"You can wear my pearl eardrops," Georgie offered.

"And my gauze shawl around your shoulders," Lady Milchamp added. "There is a laurel bush in the backyard."

"Good. Now all we require is a wig," Caroline said.

171

"A wig? Oh, my dear, I doubt there is such a thing for sale in the whole town," Lady Milchamp said. "Monsieur Dubé sells hairpieces, just a lock or two to fill out a thinning head, but a whole wig—no one wears them nowadays."

"Whoever supplies the theaters would have them," Georgie said. Her cheeks were rosy with excitement again.

"Leave it to me," Newt announced, and left to tour the town until he found either a theater or a shop selling wigs.

Georgie cleared her throat and said, "This might be a good time for you to . . . er, clean yourself up a little, Caro."

Glancing down, Caroline was surprised to see the dusty old gray gown. She had forgotten she was still in disguise. She had cast off the gloves in the carriage. Her white hands stood out in sharp contrast to her soiled arms.

"Yes," she said distractedly. She rose and looked in the mirror at her bedraggled and dusty hair sticking out around the mobcap. "I certainly do not look much like Lady Dolmain in this outfit, do I?" she asked in a wistful voice.

Lady Milchamp made a statement that went a long way to overcoming the aversion she had caused thus far. "Dolmain would not have singled you out for his attentions if you did."

It would have been too farouche to thank the lady, but Caro honored her with a warm smile.

She went to seek Mrs. Lorimer and order hot water for a bath. The housekeeper showed her to a guest room and said she would have Lorimer take up the water right away.

"I knew hot water would be needed and have both cauldrons full. Your things are laid out in the rose room, milady. Have you had any luck finding Lady Helen?" she asked hopefully.

Caroline outlined what she had discovered, and

what she meant to do. The rose room was prettily elegant. The combination of mahogany furnishings and rose lutestring window and bed hangings was a felicitous one. The walls were covered in a creamy paper dappled with roses.

After Caroline's bath, Mrs. Lorimer helped her dress and arrange Lady Milchamp's white gauze shawl in the proper fashion around her shoulders. Caro's rose shot silk did not expose as much breast as the gown in the picture, but the general effect was similar. She added Georgie's pearl eardrops.

"Now, if only Newt finds a wig," she said.

"It is nearly time for dinner, milady. Come and eat a bite first. The wig will be uncomfortable. You can put it on at the last minute. I intertwined a laurel branch with wire to make a crown of it. It turned out well."

When Caro went below, Newton had returned with a white wig he had bought in a pawnshop. The color was wrong, but the style was almost right.

"I figured at night, it might pass for blond," he said.

Lady Milchamp added, "I daresay Marie-Hélène's hair would no longer be that pretty reddish blond shade if she were alive. Not the way she lived. She would be over forty now."

Georgie shook her head. "How fleeting life is."

"And beauty," Lady Milchamp added, with a note of satisfaction. She had never been a beauty; it pleased her to see the Incomparables with whom she had made her debut sink into flesh and wrinkles, until they were no lovelier than herself.

But for Caroline, it was a sad thought. Her youth and beauty were slipping by, and with Julian gone, she had no one with whom to spend the rest of her life. More and more, she knew it was Dolmain she wanted to be with. Would he ever risk marriage again after his disastrous experience with Marie?

She pondered the incongruity of their positions. Both matches had been frowned on by the families. Yet she had had such a wonderful life with Julian that she feared she would never find anyone to replace him. Marie had shown Dolmain such a wretched time that he feared to love again. What they had in common was a wish to have a family. It seemed like fate that they had found each other. She knew he could replace Julian, but could she make him forget the faithless Marie?

She was hungry, yet did not feel like eating. The turbot in cream sauce reminded her of Renée. She wondered if they were actually trying to eat that horrid concoction she had made. She wondered, too, if Dolmain had eaten yet. He had been on the point of exhaustion when he left, hours ago. She sipped her wine, brooding as the shadows lengthened into twilight. She and Newt would not go to Bartholomew Avenue until after dark. They would watch the upper-story windows to see which room Helen went to after dinner. A light would go on, briefly at least.

"About the ladder, Caro," Newt said, drawing her from her reverie, "I discovered one in an unlocked shed at the back of the Town Hall. The outfit looks good. Did I tell you I bought some makeup to try to make your eyes look bigger? Had a word with an actress in the pawnshop. Had black lines drawn around her eyes. She says all the actresses use it to make their eyes look bigger. Pity hers was so squinty."

Lady Milchamp and Georgie carried the burden of conversation over dinner. They discussed mutual friends from the days of their debut. Caroline let the talk wash over her. It was eight o'clock. Darkness was fast closing in. Was Dolmain on his way to Brighton yet? Had he got the money rounded up? She wondered how much Bellefeuille had demanded, and hoped it was a sum Dolmain could manage.

When dinner was over she went to her bedchamber to try on the wig and to use the kohl pencil. Newt went with her. The pencil had a tendency to smudge at the slightest touch. Newton sharpened the point with his clasp knife, and she applied a line around her eyes. It lent her an exotic appearance. Then she put on the white wig, and was suddenly transformed into an old lady. She felt again that sense of urgency at time passing, at life passing her by. The crown of laurel leaves looked exactly like the one in the portrait. Perhaps it had come from the same tree. Lady Milchamp mentioned the portrait had been done in Brighton at the time of the marriage.

"Lower the lamp," Newt suggested.

She did so, and the white wig became a pale blur. She smiled the coquettish smile of the portrait. The likeness was striking enough to fool someone from a distance.

"By Jove! That's something like!" Newt said. "Why, if I didn't know you, I could fall in love with you myself."

She made a moue at him in the mirror. "Not to say that I couldn't . . . I mean . . . Oh, dash it, you know what I mean."

"Yes, I know. It is time to go, Newt." She closed her eyes and uttered a silent prayer for success.

"Take your pistol," Newt said. "The Lord helps them that help themselves."

Lady Milchamp, Georgie, and the Lorimers approved of the impersonation, wished them well, and saw them off at the door.

Lady Milchamp called from the doorway, "I just remembered something that might help, Lady Winbourne. Marie-Hélène was used to call Helen *Minou* as a pet name."

"Good, I shall call her that."

She and Newt climbed into the carriage, and were off to Bartholomew Avenue.

Lord Dolmain was not in his carriage, but mounted on a blood gray gelding, riding hell for leather toward Brighton. The ransom of fifty thousand pounds was in his saddlebag. It had taken him an hour to accumulate the sum. The majority of his funds was tied up in various investments. Fortunately, his credit was good, but if he lost that much money, things would be tight. He could hardly ask Caro to marry a man who would have to skint and save for ten years. Caro—Helen—the two cherished names and faces swirled in his brain.

He had not stopped to eat dinner. His housekeeper had made him a cold beef sandwich to take with him. He had nibbled at it when he stopped to change mounts, but couldn't swallow for the lump of anxiety in his throat. He had drunk a little wine. He didn't want to become bosky, but needed some bottled courage.

The note ordered him to place the money in the southeast corner stall of the fish market, which would be unoccupied at midnight. If he got to Brighton early enough, he could have constables or friends hiding to catch Bellefeuille as he collected the money. Of course, that was why Bellefeuille had sent the note to London and arranged the pickup in Brighton; so that he would have to scramble, leaving no time for plans.

Riding back instead of driving saved him a few hours, but it was taking its toll on his strength. Every muscle ached; he felt as if he had been marched over by an army. A note telling him where he could find Helen was supposed to be waiting for him at half past midnight at the Bull, a tavern at the west end of Brighton, well removed from the fish market, of course. Bellefeuille had added a dozen warnings. Any wavering from his orders would be instant death for Helen.

But who was to say the note would be waiting for him, or that Helen was even alive? If anything happened to her— If anything happened to Caro! No, she wouldn't do anything foolish. She had promised she would not. Losing one of the women he loved would be bad enough. If he lost them both . . .

He dug his heels into the gray's flanks, urging it on faster, faster, until he was flying through the night.

Chapter Twenty

Newton drove his carriage into the driveway of the Town Hall. He and Caro got out and peered through the bushes to Bartholomew Avenue. There were lamps burning on the ground floor of the little cottage, but none in the upper story.

"They would be dining now," Caro said.

Newt's groom, Ankel, had been conscripted to assist them. They watched the cottage for thirty minutes. Caro passed the time by describing in detail her visit to the derelict little cottage. It helped to keep her fears at bay.

At nine-thirty she said, "The dinner was to be a simple one, with plenty of wine for Helen. Half an hour seems enough time." Yet there was still no light abovestairs.

"Happen they've stashed her in a back room so's no one would spot her at the winder," Ankel suggested.

"That's it. Clever thinking, Ankel!" Caroline exclaimed.

He touched his temple. "Just using what the good Lord give me. I'll ankle along and have a peep, shall I?"

"Good lad," Newt said. "I'll get the ladder. If a guard or such comes along, Caro, you must distract him."

"How?" she asked.

"That'll be no problem," Ankel said. "He will take

you for a lightskirt. Hee hee. A painted woman out alone after dark."

"Now, see here, Ankel!" Newt blustered.

"Mind you, a very choice bit o' muslin, meaning no disrespect, milady," Ankel offered apologetically.

No guard came while the men were away. Newt was the first one back, dragging a long ladder behind him.

Ankel soon joined them. "Top left corner," he announced. "Window shut, blind drawn, a light inside."

"That's it, then," Newt said. "Take an end of this ladder, Ankel. Caro, you run into the street and see no one is about."

"They'll take us for a pair o' ken smashers," Ankel said, shaking his head and laughing. "Or are we eloping, sir? We will never live it down if word gets about. Hee hee." He slapped his thigh in appreciation of his wicked wit.

Caro went around the corner first and returned to tell them the way was clear. The street was dark, with only a fingernail of moon and a light sprinkling of stars to show the way. They kept to the shadows of a row of straggling houses that lined the street, moving so quickly that Caroline had difficulty keeping pace with them. At the cottage, they slipped along the side of the house to the rear. The ladder clattered as it was placed against the house.

At once the rear door flew open and deVere peeked out.

"Gorblimey, we're for it!" Ankel whispered.

"Who's there?" deVere called. He came pacing forward.

If he turned the corner and saw the ladder, they were done for. Emboldened by desperation, Caro walked forth into the light. She knew deVere was susceptible to women. She swung her hips and tossed her head at a coy angle.

"Just taking a shortcut, melord. I hope you don't mind." She cast a wanton smile at him. "If a girl don't get out early, all the best gents—like you—are gone," she said.

"Oh," he said, and took a step toward her, his manner friendly. She mistrusted that wolfish gleam in his eye.

Fortunately, Renée was not far behind him. "What is it, Michel?" she called from the doorway. Again, they spoke French.

"Just a lightskirt, my dear. Nothing to worry about."

"That's a matter of opinion. Come in," she called, with a scathing sneer at Caroline.

"Run along, girlie," deVere said, and reluctantly followed Renée inside as Caro hurried back to Newt and Ankel.

"You'd have found yourself warming the cove's bed if he'd been alone," Ankel said, and uttered another of his irritating *hee hee*s. "The ladder's in place. We'll hold her steady so as you don't tumble, milady." He elbowed his master in the ribs and added lecherously, "No peeking up the lady's skirt, mind."

"Behave yourself, Ankel," Newt said severely.

"Let us wait a moment to make sure deVere does not come back out," she said. She was shaken from the brief encounter with him and wanted to steady her trembling limbs.

"Do you have your pistol?" Newt asked her.

She patted the pocket of her skirt. "Right here. I hope I don't have to use it. There is no telling how this will go."

"Fear not, milady," Ankel said. "We are ready for any cattingency."

They held the ladder, and Caro looped her skirts over her arm to begin the ascent. Now that the moment had come, a strange calm possessed her. Her decision had been made, and she allowed no fears or regrets to cloud her mind. She needed all her wits for the task at hand. Heights did not bother her. It was really quite simple to climb up one story and tap at the window. She steeled herself for the light that would show when Helen opened the curtain. She waited, nothing happened. She tapped again, more loudly, gauging the pressure so that it could not be heard belowstairs. Still the curtain did not open.

Helen was asleep! They had given her enough wine to put her to sleep! Caro refused to be daunted. Helen's being asleep might be a good thing. She wouldn't be able to put up a fight, or cause a racket. Newt would have to carry her down the ladder. She was too heavy for a lady to tote. First she had to get in the window and determine that Helen was inside.

She tried to get her fingers under the window to raise it, but there wasn't so much as a quarter of an inch of space. Desperate, she knocked again, as loudly as she dared. After a short time, the curtain opened an inch. Caro tapped again, softly, now that she had the girl's attention. The curtain was pulled wide open, and a face hovered just inches away, seen through a wavy pane of glass. The light from the room beyond made the features indistinct, but the silhouette was certainly Helen's. She leapt back in astonishment, then slowly advanced to the window and gazed out. Caro smiled softly, not as the lady in the portrait smiled, but with love and yearning, as a mother should smile at her long-lost daughter. Helen continued looking at her with unbelieving eyes for a minute that seemed an eternity, then drew open the window.

"Mama! Is it really you?" she asked, in French.

Caro replied, "Minou, *je suis revenue à toi, enfin.*"

"Oh, Mama!" Helen reached through the window and threw her arms around Caro's neck. The ladder jiggled precariously.

"Viens, viens vite, ma chère!" Caro said urgently.

Helen drew back. "Oh, Mama, you did not have to come by the window!" she said, laughing. "Lord deVere is our friend." She stared at Caro again, her eyes moving over the white wig, then to the face. "You look so young!" Then her pretty little face clenched in anger. "You are not Mama! You are Lady Winbourne." She reached to slam the window, at the same time turning her head toward the door to shout for help.

Caroline's perch atop the ladder was insecure. She had few options, and neither arguing nor explaining was amongst them. She threw her upper body through the window, her hips resting on the ledge, and made a grab for Helen, catching her by the hair. Caught off guard, Helen fell against the window. Caroline drew out the pistol and pointed it at her.

"One word and I'll shoot," she said. She climbed in the window, pointing the gun at Helen all the while. Caro was sorry the rescue had taken this harsh turn; she had hoped to lure Helen out in a civilized manner, but the girl's life was at stake, and mere etiquette must not ruin her rescue.

Helen was frightened but also angry. Sparks of fire shot from her eyes. "What do you want?" she demanded.

"You are coming with me."

"I will not! I shall call Lord deVere."

"I am not fooling, Lady Helen. I will shoot anyone who comes through that door to help you. Now, get out that window." She felt her best weapon was intimidation, and although she was sorry, she did not hesitate to use it, for any show of uncertainty would be quickly taken advantage of.

Helen stared at her in disdain. "You can't make me. Go ahead, shoot me—if you dare."

Caroline had not thought the girl would have the courage to call her bluff. She was at point nonplus.

"Don't be an idiot!" she said. "DeVere is not your friend. He is using you."

"Why should I listen to you? You're a common thief."

"Shut up, you foolish girl!" Caro's pent-up nerves could no longer be controlled. "We know you gave the necklace to deVere. Your stupidity has cost your father a diamond necklace and may well cost him his life before this night is over. It is your dowry that will pay for your ransom, miss. How will you like being penniless?"

"I would gladly give my money to rescue Mama. And Papa would gladly give the necklace, too. He loves her."

In desperation, Caro decided to tell Helen the whole truth. She had to know it sooner or later, and it seemed the only way to get her to leave. "No, *you* love her, because you don't know the first thing about her. She ran off on your papa—and you— with another man. Monsieur Bellefeuille, whom you call deVere. Dolmain kept it from you to protect your innocence. Well, you are no longer so innocent."

Helen's face tensed in denial. "It's not true! Mama was working in France, risking her life. Papa only thought she was dead. DeVere found her."

"He did not find her. She is dead. She drowned in a storm off Weymouth half a dozen years ago. I am sorry to be the bearer of bad news, but it's time you knew the truth. DeVere was holding you to ransom. He plans to get more money from your father. Dolmain is in London now arranging it."

"You're lying. You just want Papa to marry you. Mama is alive. She is, she *is*." She stamped her foot in vexation.

"Hush! They will hear us." Caro brandished the gun again, desperately trying to get Helen to leave without creating a disturbance that would bring deVere rushing upstairs.

The girl was young and wiry, and too close to her own size to compel her physically without making a good deal of racket. The only thing she could think of was to knock her out, drag her to the window, and call for Newt to come up and help her. She stood a moment, gathering her fortitude for this course.

Chapter Twenty-one

As Dolmain darted through the blackness of night toward Brighton, his mind wandered over the past, regretting his brief and bitter alliance with Marie-Hélène. Except for Helen, no good had come of it. Marie, an angel before she snared him, had been trouble from the day he married her—and a conniving deceiver before that, although he was too young and besotted by her beauty and her tantalizing sexual expertise to realize it. He should have suspected when she talked him into buying that cottage on Bartholomew Avenue just a week before their wedding. "For my cousins to go on living in," she had said, with a doleful sigh. "They are not so fortunate as I, *mon cher*. I have you. I want to share my joy with them."

But he had learned the Drouins with whom she had been living were no kin to her. It had been a plot to get a thousand pounds from him, while painting herself as Lady Bountiful. She had bought the house; she proudly showed him the ownership papers. Two years later, she had sold it to a boot-maker—or so she said. He had never cared enough to look into it. It was possible she had kept it for a trysting spot with her lovers. Bellefeuille might know of it. . . .

Helen claimed French émigrés still lived there. How had she learned about the house? He had never told her exactly where Marie lived before he married her. He hadn't mentioned Marie at all, except when Helen asked a direct question, yet she knew the house. Lady Milchamp, perhaps, had pointed it out to her. Of course Helen would go to view this shrine. Had she met Bellefeuille there?

It was not in Marie's nature to give anything away, including her love. She had a great respect for property. She had probably not sold the house at all, but rented it to some French friends. In her will, she had left what she possessed to Bellefeuille. He might now be the owner of the house. If so, it was the logical place to take Helen. As it was not far out of his way, Dolmain decided to investigate. He had made good time; he could spare a few minutes.

He felt a sense of revulsion when he rode past the familiar cottage, the scene of his youthful folly. Lights were lit in the downstairs parlor, which was strange, for the house had an air of long neglect. Even by moonlight he could see the paint on the door and around the windows had weathered and peeled. The roof sagged, the garden was overgrown. Someone was making use of the house for only a short while, then, a sort of emergency stop. A tingle whispered up his spine.

He rode around the corner, looking for a place to tether his mount. There were tethering posts at the Town Hall. He dismounted and tied his reins to the post, unfastened the saddlebag holding the money and took it with him. It would be disastrous to lose the ransom money.

He walked swiftly back around the corner to the cottage. The shades were drawn in the parlor, so he went around to the back to see if any lamps burned there. As he turned the corner, he saw the ladder leaning against the house, and stopped dead. What could this mean? A derelict cottage was not the sort of house thieves burgled. Had he stumbled into an elopement? He secreted the saddlebag in the bushes, went to the ladder, looked all around, and put his foot on the bottom rung.

When Newton and Ankel heard his approach, they feared deVere had turned suspicious and come out to check. Their first instinct had been self-preservation. They darted behind the tangled hedge that separated the house from its neighbor. Once they were safe, common sense returned.

"We can't let him crawl up there. He might harm Caro," Newt whispered.

"Is it the bleater that stole her ladyship?" Ankel whispered back.

"Could be. It's tall enough. Whoever it is, he's up to no good. Thing to do, we'll let him get well up the ladder, then yank it out from under him."

"He'll bust a leg. Hee hee. That'll slow down his chase of the ladies. Best get moving. He's scampering up pretty fast."

What had impelled Dolmain to increase his speed was the sound of voices coming from the open window. Helen's voice! His heart pounded in mingled fear and joy.

"You're lying!" Helen said. "I'm not going with you. You're not my mother."

Dolmain clamped his hands over the window ledge, just as Ankel and Newton jerked the ladder out from under him. He managed to brace his foot against the wall until he could heave himself onto the window ledge. He leapt into the room, staring wildly at the incredible scene before him.

Fatigue, fear, anger, and confusion clouded his mind. He saw Marie, come back from the dead, trying to steal Helen from him. It was his worst nightmare. She cared nothing for Helen, but she often used her as a pawn, threatening to lure her away. That wreath of vines in her hair, the white rolled shawl he had seen scores of times in the portrait— she had not drowned at Weymouth after all. It had been a trick. Marie's body had scarcely been recognizable after two days in the water. It was Bellefeuille who identified her by her clothing. Bellefeuille had found some woman who resembled Marie. . . .

When he spoke, his voice betrayed no doubt or hesitation. "Drop that gun, Marie, or I will—"

The wreathed head turned to face him, and the nightmare turned to madness. Caro! Oh God, it was Caro who had stolen the diamonds—and kidnapped his daughter. He, blinded by love again, had taken her into his complete confidence, into his heart. He felt as if a mountain had fallen on him.

"Dolmain! Thank God you are here!" the vision said, and rushed to him with her arms open in welcome.

He pushed her off with a stiff arm and a stern face. Did she take him for a complete idiot? He spoke in the hollow voice of despair. "So it was you, all the time. I will see you hang from the gibbet for this, Lady Winbourne."

Caro stared in disbelief, beyond words.

Helen pitched herself into his arms. "Oh, Papa, she said the worst things! She said Mama did not love us, that she ran away and left us."

"You told my daughter that!" he exclaimed.

"She refused to come with me, Dolmain. And I wish you will lower your voice, for Bellefeuille is downstairs." She heard a noise outside the door. "Hush! Oh God, he is coming!"

Bellefeuille had heard the ladder falling, seen it lying on the ground, and feared someone had come to rescue Helen. He darted quickly upstairs to take her away. The first indication of his approach was a running patter outside the door, then at once the door was thrown open and he entered, holding a pistol. A sneering smile disfigured his face as he glanced from Helen to Dolmain, scarcely noticing Caroline.

"So, we meet again, milord!" he said.

Caro quietly lowered her right arm, concealing her pistol in the folds of her skirt. No one was paying her any heed.

Dolmain felt a recrudescence of all the shame and misery this man and Marie had caused him. "You son of a bitch, I'll tear you limb from limb!" he growled, and flew at Bellefeuille.

Bellefeuille saw the rage in his eyes. He knew Dolmain was too enraged to fear for his own life, but he would never endanger his daughter's. He stepped aside as Dolmain lunged at him. Helen was only six inches away. He grabbed her by the arm and pulled her in front of him.

"Take care, milord. It would be a shame to have to kill your daughter," he said in a voice of silken menace.

Dolmain saw the terror in Helen's eyes as she was wrenched in front of Bellefeuille. He knew the muzzle of the gun was pressed against her spine, and he froze. How could he direct Bellefeuille's anger against himself, to allow Helen to escape?

"Hiding behind a lady's skirts, Bellefeuille?" he taunted. "This is between you and me. Put your pistol aside and fight like a man—if you are a man."

"A pity your wife is dead, or you could ask her," Bellefeuille laughed.

Helen turned around to stare at Bellefeuille. "Dead? You said Mama was alive! You said you had found her!"

Bellefeuille's eyes never left Dolmain's as he replied. "You served my purpose equally well, *ma petite.*"

The tension in the room was like a palpable presence. The men were concentrating on each other, with Helen between them. Helen's abrupt movement left Bellefeuille's right side exposed. Caro saw her opportunity. She must make no sudden movement to alert him, yet she must quickly raise her gun and shoot him, without injuring Helen. If Bellefeuille realized what she was up to, he would not hesitate to shoot her.

"You lied to me!" Helen said, and moved a little way from her captor to turn around and accuse him.

Bellefeuille reached to grab her back. Fearing for her life, Dolmain said, "It's all right, Helen."

In the brief instant they were thus occupied, Caro raised her pistol, took fast aim, and shot Bellefeuille in the right shoulder. The shot reverberated in the small room like a cannon going off. Chaos ensued. Bellefeuille dropped his gun and let off a string of curses, grabbing his wounded shoulder. Dolmain cast one startled glance at Caro, then darted forward and grabbed the gun from the floor. Helen stared from one of them to the other, then burst into tears.

"He had Helen. I came to try to rescue her," Caro said.

"But why are you wearing—" He looked at her disguise and shook his head in confusion.

As they stood, staring at each other, Newt's head popped up at the window like a jack-in-the-box. "Oh, it's you, Dolmain. That's all right, then." He climbed into the chamber and dusted himself off. "See you've winged your man. Best get him off to the roundhouse, eh? Caro can take Helen home. Don't want the ladies mixed up in a shooting match."

Dolmain, in the aftermath of the near-tragedy and at the end of an extremely strenuous day, seemed to have lost his wits. He stood, looking from one to the other in confusion.

"Yes, let us go," Caro said. "Oh, and you won't forget Renée, Newt. She is belowstairs."

Newt looked out the window. "She ain't, you know. She is making a run for it. Ah, Ankel has nabbed her. Good lad, Ankel." He stuck his head out the window and called down, "Tie her up right and tight. We will be down presently."

Helen turned a tearful face to her father. "Papa, is it true, what Lady Winbourne said?"

"Your mother ran away with her lover," he said simply. "I should have told you. I'm sorry, my dear, but you still have your old papa." He turned to Caro. "Thanks to Lady Winbourne," he added with a strange, haunted look. How could he ever have mistaken her for Marie, even for an instant? Yet in the wig and that gown, there was an uncanny resemblance. She was what he had thought Marie was. The same liveliness and *joie de vivre* and beauty, without the selfishness and lack of morals.

"Thing to do," Newt said. "Continue this chat later, after we have got deVere booked. Bleeding like a stuck pig. Daresay he will need a sawbones," he added, with a glance at the man who was holding his right shoulder with his left hand. Blood oozed between his fingers.

Newt led the way downstairs. Caro gave Helen a gentle shove after him. She went readily enough now that Dolmain was there. Caro followed behind, with Dolmain going last, in a state of rising euphoria as the facts fell into place. It was over. Helen was safe. And Caro had not scratched his eyes out for his attack on her. How could he have suspected Caro?

He stopped her at the top of the stairs and said in a stricken voice, "My darling, can you ever forgive me?"

"Later, Dolmain. I shall take Helen home while you and Newt deal with Bellefeuille and Renée."

His fingers squeezed hers so hard, her hands ached. A flash sparked from his dark eyes. "And then I shall return to Marine Parade and deal with *you*, my sweet liar. You might have got yourself

191

killed! You *promised* me you would not—and thank you, with all my heart, for paying me no heed."

"I was afraid you would not be back in time. You must have ridden both ways." She gazed at his dear, haggard face, then lifted her hand and placed her palm against his cheek.

"I did, *ventre à terre.*"

She felt such a rush of love when he smiled at her like that. "You look worn to the socket," she scolded.

"I never felt better in my life," he said, and held her closely against him a moment, with his forehead leaning on hers, reveling in the knowledge that Caro and his daughter were safe, that Caro must truly love him, or why had she taken such frightening risks? He would have nightmares about these hours. Then he lifted his head and smiled wanly at her. "I don't deserve you. You risked your life, and I was afraid to risk my heart. What a laggard you must think me."

"No, that is not how you appear to me."

"Are you coming, Papa?" Helen called.

They moved apart and continued downstairs, and on out to the carriage. Dolmain stopped only to retrieve his saddlebag containing the money from the bushes. That would go back in the bank now. Ankel, to his deep dismay, was commissioned to drive the ladies home in Newt's carriage while Newt and Dolmain did what they had to do with Bellefeuille and Renée. They allowed Bellefeuille to ride Dolmain's mount to the roundhouse as he was weak from his wound, but Dolmain held the bridle. Renée spat out such a hail of vituperation on Bellefeuille that one could almost pity him. Almost.

In the carriage, Helen sat bent over with her head in her lap, sniffling quietly into her hands. Caro knew she was suffering; to all intents and purposes, the mother she had idolized for a decade had died that night in a little room on Bartholomew Avenue. Caro feared anything she could say would only make matters worse. She just patted Helen's shoulder.

As they approached Marine Parade, Helen sat up and said in an apologetic tone, "Was deVere—he called himself deVere—going to keep the money from Mama's necklace? And were you really rescuing me?"

"Yes. I am sorry I had to threaten you, but I feared you would alert Bellefeuille that I was there."

"How could Mama have run off with him? He is horrid." Caro felt a small, warm hand pressing its way into hers. "Thank you, Lady Winbourne. I am sorry for . . . you know, everything," Helen said. "You are very brave. Papa does not really think you are a thief. He likes you."

Caro patted her hand. "I know, my dear. I know."

"I liked you, too. It was just that I feared if Papa fell in love with you, he would not want Mama back, you see."

"I understand."

Helen felt she ought to say more, but she sensed that Lady Winbourne was not really attending to her. She was holding her hand tightly, though, as if she did not despise her. It felt good, warm and safe. Lady Winbourne was very courageous. She had fired that pistol without a quiver. And she was pretty, too. Everyone admired her style. It would be wonderful to be like her. How could she make sure that Papa married her?

Chapter Twenty-two

"Why did you not tell me the truth before, Papa?" Helen demanded when Dolmain and Newton returned to Marine Parade an hour later.

Was she growing up on him, or were ladies born knowing that offense is the best defense? In any case, Dolmain was happy to see his daughter sitting beside Caro, courting her. *Courting* seemed the proper word for the shyly smiling manner in which Helen behaved. She filled Caro's glass before it was half-empty, and arranged her shawl solicitously although it was not the least chilly in the room.

"I wish I had," he said, ruffling her curls. "I felt you were too young to be exposed to the harsh truth."

"I am not a child!"

She looked remarkably like one to her fond papa. "It would have saved a deal of trouble if I had told you, would it not?"

"Did you get the Dolmain necklace back?" Helen asked. She had always called it "Mama's necklace" before. He took this for a sign Marie was receding into the past, where she belonged.

"Yes, Bellefeuille had not sold it yet. He had pried out the diamonds to sell separately, to avoid detection. The major jewelers would have recognized the necklace. I shall have it restyled when— later." His eyes flickered to Caro, who had removed the wig and gauze collar.

He liked her much better as herself. Now that

the ordeal was over, he felt he could come to terms even with Marie's duplicity. One day he would be able to forgive her. Her life had not been easy before marrying him, and she had paid the ultimate price for her sins. Then, too, she had given him Helen.

"How much money did Bellefeuille demand for Helen's return?" Lady Milchamp inquired. He could hardly drag his eyes away from Caro. He wished everyone would leave, so that they could be alone together.

"Fifty thousand. I had to hop through hoops to get it. You can thank Caro for saving your dot, Helen. Such a shatterbrained creature as you would have uphill work finding a husband without a good dowry."

Helen smiled demurely at Caro. "Thank you, Lady Winbourne. I am truly sorry for all the bother I caused. I never dreamed you would be accused of taking the necklace. It was your sitting beside me in Lady Castlereagh's parlor that put the notion in everyone's head. And after people did begin to suspect you, I felt it would be all right in the end, because after Mama came back, everyone would know what had really happened to the diamonds, and that you were innocent. It is quite romantic to be wrongly accused, don't you think?"

"Charming," Caro said, with a peek at Dolmain, who winced.

"When Bellefeuille said that he needed more money for the trip to Paris, I decided to give him the emerald brooch," Helen continued. "As you were with me that day, it looked as if you had taken it, too. If Papa had only told me the truth—"

"I shall never hear the end of that," Dolmain said tolerantly. He was too happy to give his daughter the scold she deserved, but he meant to keep a closer eye on her in future. She was too young to make her debut. He would take her back to

Elmhurst until next year, and knock some sense into her.

"I accept your apology, Helen," Caro said. "What is done is done. Let us not make a meal of it. I am more interested to learn how you notified Bellefeuille that you were leaving London, and would meet him at Reigate."

"The servants knew nothing of it," Dolmain said.

"I did not use a servant," Helen said. "Miss Blanchard used to take messages, and when she was killed, I just watched for Pierre from my bedroom window, and threw notes to him. I wrote that we would be stopping at Reigate overnight, and that I would await word there. I knew they would come."

"What happened to Bellefeuille and Renée, Dolmain?" Caroline asked. "And who is Renée, exactly?"

"She is Bellefeuille's wife of one year. Newt and I led the pair of them off to the magistrate. They are warming a cell in the roundhouse overnight, and will be formally charged in the morning. Bellefeuille has had his eye on my wallet ever since Marie's death. It was his meeting Miss Blanchard at one of those French émigré meetings that put the notion of using Helen into his head. Blanchard told him Helen did not know the truth about Marie, and she encouraged my daughter to idolize her mama, with the intention of later saying Marie was alive, and required a grand sum of money for her rescue from Paris. Why did you not tell me what was afoot, Helen?" he asked, turning to frown at his daughter.

"They said it would be dangerous for you to be involved when you were active at the Horse Guards in the fight against the French. That it might be misunderstood, and the Cabinet would suspect you of spying or some such thing. I was a fool to believe them." She scowled.

"Next time you are in doubt, talk to me," Dolmain said.

"She is young," Lady Milchamp said forgivingly.

"I wanted so badly to believe it was true," Helen said. She looked so forlorn that no one chided her further.

Dolmain continued his story. "Miss Blanchard was induced by greed to go along with stealing the necklace, but when Bellefeuille escalated the affair to kidnapping Helen, she dug in her heels and refused. She did care for Helen, after her fashion. She foolishly threatened Bellefeuille that she was going to tell me, instead of doing it. That was when he shot her. She had acquired the habit of taking Rex for a walk at night. I fancy those walks were used to exchange messages with Bellefeuille. He arranged to meet her to pick up the brooch Helen had given Miss Blanchard. The strange thing is, he insists he did not get the brooch from her. Someone was coming, and he had to leave before getting it. It is odd he would stick at that trifle when he has admitted to all the rest."

"He didn't get it. Crumm did," Newt said, and explained in his disjointed fashion Crumm's part in the affair.

"I meant to tell you," Caro said, "but things got so lively after that that the moment never seemed right. I wished Crumm had left it where it was."

"It made no odds in the long run," Dolmain said. He felt her subterfuge was his fault. If he had not ripped up at her at the ball, she would not have had to defend herself.

"Killing Miss Blanchard meant one less to share the booty," Dolmain continued. "Bernard was no relation to her, by the by. He was one of Bellefeuille's gang. Renée spilled the whole story. Word has been sent to Bow Street to round the rest of them up. They have not even the excuse of acting for their country. It was not a scheme to get money to help

197

Boney—they are French, that could be forgiven—but pure greed."

"What did they plan to do with me after they got the money, Papa?" Helen asked.

"They would hardly admit they planned to kill you," he said, using the harsh truth to frighten her into more sensible behavior in future. "They said they meant to release you. I take leave to doubt it. You could identify them."

Helen trembled to consider the fate planned for her. "And deVere seemed so nice. He gave me anything I asked for. Little things, I mean, like cream tarts and magazines."

"Well paid for at fifty thousand pounds and a diamond necklace," her father pointed out.

"Beware of Greeks bearing gifts," Newt said wisely.

"He was not a Greek, Mr. Newton," Helen said.

"Foreigner anyhow. All Greek to me, as the saying goes."

"That is not what the saying means," she said, laughing.

He was beginning to think Lady Helen was not quite the thing after all. Bound to be a handful, like her mama. He really hadn't time to court a lady, just at the moment. There was a deal of work to be done on his epic. *The Round Table Rondeau*, he would call it. Had a nice ring to it, except that the dictionary told him a rondeau had only ten or thirteen lines, which was pretty short for an epic. He would have to write up a batch of them. *Round Table Rondeaus*, then, or would the French word have an *x* on the end? *Round Table Rondeaux?* Rum touch, the Frenchies. Terrible spellers.

"What is the plural of rondeau anyway?" he asked. The group around him blinked in confusion. "Never mind. I was thinking of my epic. Well, if we have got everything tied up here, I shall be off.

Booked a room at the Royal Crescent. Ankel will want to hear all the details."

"Drop around tomorrow, Newt," Caro said, and rose to accompany him to the door.

Dolmain and Helen thanked him profusely for his help. "My pleasure," he said, and nodded his head stiffly. He hadn't discovered yet just how a bow was performed in King Arthur's day, but he felt that a knight would make little of his deeds of derring-do. He meant to pitch himself into the thing whole hog. He left.

"What a funny little man he is," Helen said, and yawned into her fist.

The older ladies felt the strain of their long day, too. Lady Milchamp rose and said, "Time for bed, miss." She looked a question at Dolmain.

"Caro and I shall have a drink to celebrate the successful conclusion of this affair. Don't wait up for us. We have a good deal to talk about."

Georgiana cast an encouraging smile on Caro. Dolmain would be a fine catch. It had been a nice little adventure, but she was ready to go home. Meanwhile, she had found a marble-covered novel in the library here that would lull her to sleep.

Helen ran to kiss her papa good night. She looked at Caro, then, on impulse, kissed her, too, and ran out of the room at once, as if frightened by her own temerity.

Dolmain turned to Caro. "I don't know whether to begin with apologies, or thanks, or a scold."

"Do get the scold over first, by all means." Smiling, she brushed her cheek where Helen had kissed her. That had come as a complete surprise. She should have returned the kiss.

"Consider yourself scolded—and thanked—and apologized to, most humbly. I can never thank you enough."

"You are welcome, Dolmain. I shan't quote Newt and say, 'My pleasure,' but it was exciting."

"It was that. Now let us get on to the good part. Caro, I want to make it up to you."

She turned a rebellious eye on him. "Don't you dare offer to marry me to redeem my reputation!"

"Oh no! *That* is not why I am offering. The reputations that will require redemption when this scandal breaks are Helen's—and mine, for being such a fool as to keep her in the dark all these years."

"Misguided paternal concern," she said, forgivingly. "You men always think you know what is best for us ladies."

"No more, but I do know what is best for me. You! I have not felt so whole, so complete, for years." He gazed at her softly, not touching her, except with his eyes. "I truly do not think I could go on without you. God, how selfish love makes us. Here am I prating of my feelings, when I should be concerned with yours."

She smiled demurely. "You men are all selfish beasts. I know it very well."

"Don't be difficult, woman," he said, drawing her into his arms, and closer against his chest until their bodies touched. "You know I love you to the edge of distraction," he said in a ragged voice. "Your foolish behavior this night leads me to believe you are not totally disinterested in my welfare."

"There was Helen, and my own reputation to consider as well," she said, gazing at him. She felt humbled by the love she read in his eyes.

"Ah, Helen." He placed a small kiss on first one eye, then the other. "You cannot anticipate living with her with anything like complacence." A frown wrinkled his brow. She felt an overpowering need to smooth it away.

"Nonsense!" she said gruffly, drawing back. "Helen and I go on very well now that she knows I was only trying to help her. She needs watching, and a little more time to mature before she is sent off to choose a husband, though."

He pulled her roughly back into his arms. "Exactly what I thought. Another year at Elmhurst, with some sensible lady to model herself after. Never having known a real mother, she has a craving for one, I think. There is no point fighting it, my pet." His lips nuzzled her throat. "We have both chosen you."

Her speech came out breathlessly. "In that case, I suppose it is unanimous."

Dolmain lifted his eyes to the ceiling and whispered, "Thank you, God." He drew her into his arms and ravished her with a long kiss.

It did not occur to Caro, when she went to bed much later that night, that Julian's portrait was not there to talk to. Like Marie, he was beginning to recede into the mist of memory. She thought of dear Dolmain, and Helen, and how she could make them happy.